Sarah Dunes,
Weird Person

Sarah Dunes, Weird Person

Lois I. Fisher

DODD, MEAD & COMPANY / New York

Copyright © 1981 by Lois I. Fisher
All rights reserved
No part of this book may be reproduced in any form
without permission in writing from the publisher
Printed in the United States of America

1   2   3   4   5   6   7   8   9   10

Library of Congress Cataloging in Publication Data

Fisher, Lois I
Sarah Dunes, weird person.

SUMMARY: It takes a lot before Sarah, a 13-year-old
goalie, discovers that she isn't as weird as she thought.
[1. Hockey—Fiction]   I. Title.
PZ7.F5338Sar   [Fic]   80-2780
ISBN 0-396-07929-6

To Mama and Dad, for their support.

1

I hopped over the boards and skated across the rink. "Way to go!" I shouted. The ice was filled with deliriously happy Blue Dolphins, all decked out in navy-colored uniforms and white helmets. Except I don't have a helmet; I'm the spare goalie, you see, and mainly, I get to carry around my terrific looking zigzag white-and-blue mask.

Steve Hollaway, the first-string goalie, had played a super game, shutting out the tough Jets. We all pounded him on the back, congratulated each other, then left the ice. Most of the Dolphins headed in one direction; Piggy Barnes and I walked in the other.

I shoved open the door to the girl's locker room. As usual, I forgot about the shiny tiles and skidded across the room. I braced myself against the nearest locker and said, "Fantastic game, Piggy! That shorthanded goal you scored was something else! The way you deked . . ."

Piggy plunked down on a splintery bench and spit. "I always play great, Sarah Dunes."

Piggy's going to enter the Miss America Pageant and

win the Miss Congeniality Award—if she doesn't, she'll mug the judges. I *had* wanted to ask her how she'd missed two point-blank shots on a power play but I decided to play it safe and take a shower. Actually, since I didn't play, I didn't need one but *maybe* Piggy would get the hint. She didn't.

When I came out of the too-cold shower, Coach Caplan was there. She's actually the assistant coach but she knows more about the game than the head guy, Mr. Darrow. He's okay but he raves on about players like Andy Bathgate and Maurice Richard. Goodies, sure, but oldies! I don't think he'd recognize my hero, Olympic gold medalist Jim Craig (I have pictures of him all over my room), if he fell over him.

"The whole team played so well!" Coach Caplan said.

"Yeah, I did a great job of warming up," I said, tugging on my tee shirt. The shirt is a reject of my dad's; he's tall and skinny, too.

"Now, Sarah, you'll get your chance."

"I know. It really doesn't bother me. Steve's the best goalie around. I don't mind taking a back seat." *True!* There isn't any discrimination on the Dolphins. Piggy's our star right-winger. And I beat out three boys for the second-string job. Sure, I'd rather play all the time. Who wouldn't? But being part of the team pleases me, even if my best friends, Connie Russo and Gayle Steinberg, think I'm weird. Connie always tells me to try out for track.

"You won't get killed doing that, Sarah."

"I'm not going to get killed playing hockey."

"But you could lose your teeth. And what boy wants to kiss a girl with false teeth?"

Connie nags me about that. Okay, the idea of wearing dentures doesn't thrill me. But I don't worry about it, which is probably why I'm Sarah Dunes, Weird Person.

My Aunt Rhonda is another one who thinks I'm crazy to be backup goalie. The key word is *backup*. Rhonda's a devout feminist. If I don't get to be number one, she thinks I'm being discriminated against.

"We play the Tornadoes next, Sarah. I'm sure you'll get in against them. At Monday's workout, we'll go over their roster."

"Terrific, Coach," I said, zipping up my jacket. "See ya, Piggy."

She grunted.

It was dark already and the wind was blowing like mad. I live in the coldest nook of Dutchess County, New York. When I lived in New York City, the weather never seemed this cold, unless I was walking through the Bronx Zoo.

Connie and Gayle were waiting for me. Connie's one of those tiny girls, all hair and no face. She makes up for her small stature by a big mouth. Gayle, who's really pretty, used to make a lot of noise, too, but she's been incredibly quiet since she came back from a Halloween weekend in the Adirondacks.

"You didn't play again! I'm spending my entire allowance watching violent hockey games and you don't even put in an appearance!" Connie yelled.

I shrugged and glanced at Gayle. The lights from the schoolyard caught her face. Her huge blue eyes had a far-away look. I wondered if she had a fight with David, a boy she dates. I didn't ask; if she wanted to, she'd tell me.

"Let's get thick shakes," Connie said. "The Dairy Queen's having a special this week."

"No. I have to get home," Gayle said flatly.

I stared at her. Gayle never *had to* get home. Her folks never minded what she did. Connie thinks that's because Gayle's an only child. Well, I'm one, too, and you should hear the screaming that takes place at my house if I'm more than ten minutes late!

"Sounds yummy," I said, "but mom's working late so dad and I have to cook." My mother's the newly appointed manager of the local Greymer & Greymer department store; Greymer is like Saks and Bergdorf's, only nicer.

"Did you try the manicotti recipe I gave you?"

Connie's the world's best cook. She can take nothing and make it into a feast. "I gave it to mom," I replied. "She'll try it some Sunday."

We said good-bye at the next corner. Gayle lives at the end of Collier Lane, where the "old" houses are. Connie's house is two blocks over, in the Regency Townhouse development. I think the RTs are okay but dad says they're good for termite sandwiches and not much else. And he should know; he's a part-time realtor. He's actually the best cartoonist around but he has to make a living somehow, until everyone agrees with my opinion of his work.

Our house isn't old or a bug-sandwich. It's a one-of-a-kind, which means it stands out like a tight end in a tutu. When I opened the door, I shouted, "Hello there!"

And was promptly howled at by Sir Lancelot, our gray tiger cat. I'm going to get a dog as soon as hockey season ends. Wonder how Sir L will feel about that? We found him huddled and starving on the back porch a week after we moved in last fall. Dad swore he hated cats but I begged to take him in. Our city apartment had had a "No Pets Allowed" rule.

I almost lost Sir L after taking him in. He wouldn't eat and he really seemed sick. We took him to a vet and found out he had some awful cat disease. The vet gave him shots and prescribed pills. I was so scared he'd die on me. I spent hours in the kitchen with Sir L (the warmest spot in the house), feeding him what little he would eat by hand and giving him his medicine. And when I wasn't in the kitchen with him, I was sitting on the cool, bathroom tiles worrying about him. I was really overjoyed when he pulled through and gave me the first of many slashes.

In fact, he was clawing at my jeans right now and howling to be fed.

"Hi, Sarah!" Dad hollered.

"Dad's home—you were already fed," I said to Sir L. I pried his paws off me; he hissed and darted under the couch. I walked into the kitchen where dad was. His sweat shirt was splattered with tomato sauce. He always stirs too hard.

"Did you win?"

"Yeah, Steve shut them out five-zip."

"I take it you didn't get a chance to play? Tell me how this tastes." He pushed a wooden spoon in front of my face.

"I'll burn my tongue. Besides, you *know* I'll say there isn't enough basil. There's *never* enough basil!"

"Mmmm." He took a jar down from the spice rack. "You didn't answer my first question, Sarah."

"I didn't get in but will the next time."

"That means you'll be playing that dreadful team, the Tornadoes."

"Right. Any calls?"

"None for you. Rhonda called, though. She'll be here Sunday."

I didn't offer to help with the sauce or the meatballs. Cooking isn't my forte. Except for boiling water. I'm good at that because I love to drink instant cocoa and herbal tea. So, I put the huge copper pot on for spaghetti.

"Not so much salt!" Dad yelled, grabbing the shaker from me. "If we wanted ocean water, we could've hauled it up from the city last year!"

"Aw, you spoil all my fun."

"If one more prospective Santa comes in drunk. . . ."

I ran out of the kitchen and kissed mom. Her glasses

were fogged up; she took them off and I helped her find a chair (she's blind without her specs). Then she loosened the collar of her tweed coat.

"Honestly! Bombed Santa applicants! Thought they'd stop once we left the city."

I handed her back her defogged glasses. "I read somewhere that there are more alcoholics in the suburbs—"

Mom batted her thick eyelashes at me. "You read it, Sarah? What hockey magazine, sports magazine, or collection of *Charlie Brown* comic strips told you that enlightening fact?"

I sighed. Mom doesn't approve of my reading matter. She wants me to read big, fat, thick books. I have a theory; if a book is over three hundred pages and has a rough feeling cover that's either maroon or hunter green, the book is either boring or simply smarter than I am. So I stick to magazines, books about dogs and cats, and sports biographies.

"I beg your pardon, Sarah. You also read those ghastly fan magazines. I do imagine some rock singers are heavy drinkers but I can't imagine such a magazine doing research on alcoholics in the suburbs—"

"Okay, maybe I *heard* it on TV."

"—those magazines are mainly concerned with what kind of acne cream Superstar A uses or what kind of toothpaste—which reminds me, Sarah, you have a dentist's appointment tomorrow at eleven."

13

2

We sat down for dinner and mom still rattled on about drunken St. Nicks. "I asked him about his previous employment and he said, 'Hic, the Easter Bunny, Toots.'"

We laughed; mom *hates* to be called Toots.

"How come you interviewed him?" I asked, twirling the endless spaghetti skein around my bent fork. "I thought you were a big shot at Greymer."

"Big shot, little shot. The store is in such a state of confusion that it doesn't make any difference. I'll even have to work Saturdays with the Christmas season starting."

"Christmas? Mom, Thanksgiving hasn't happened yet."

"So?"

"So, aren't you rushing the season a little?"

"*I'm* rushing it?" Mom laughed, choked on a meatball and downed some Uncola. "What about the sports season? Seems like the World Series just ended and you've already

14

played two hockey games. And your father has married the football—"

"Truce!" Dad interrupted. "We'll need one. Rhonda's coming over Sunday."

I watched mom's face. I know she loves her younger sister but there's a pained look she gets every time Rhonda is supposed to come over, which makes me wonder if you can love and hate a person at the same time. Rhonda's our only close relative nearby, however. Mom has another sister, Rosiland, who's older (in business for herself and divorced twice). We don't see much of her because she lives in Florida; we only see her every-other-Christmas— *this* Christmas will be an every-other! There's dad's brother, Harry. I remember him being great but he took his family to Texas six years ago and we haven't seen them since.

That's why Rhonda is special. Even if mom looks pained.

"I wonder if she's still out of work?" Mom said.

"Her unemployment benefits should be running out soon," Dad said.

"That's what I'm going to be when I'm older."

"Huh?" They asked together.

"Unemployed."

They laughed. I thought about what I'd just said. It was true; at the rate I come up with career possibilities, unemployment seems like the best bet.

Take Connie—she's going to be anchor woman on a network news program. She *knows* that. And Gayle is pretty much set on becoming a doctor. Either that or a research scientist. At least they're connected fields!

I walked over to the fridge to get dessert. Betcha even Piggy Barnes has her life planned out. Which leaves only me, Sarah Dunes, Weird Person, without a blueprint.

After eating two helpings of chocolate ice cream, I called Gayle. "Hi, it's me. Got a dentist appointment in the village tomorrow. Want to come along?"

"I'm sorry, Sarah. I can't make it."

I wanted to ask, "Why not?" But I sensed she wouldn't give me a straight answer.

What could be bothering Gayle? After I hung up, I wondered. David? Yeah. Only a boy could cause someone to act like that. I've never had boyfriend problems. Oh, there's Alex Smythe. We went to a few parties together last spring but he's lost interest in me this semester. Although I'd like to know why, it isn't one of my top-ten pressing problems.

My parents had left the kitchen and were now in the living room. There isn't a wall between the two rooms. They kind of blend into each other.

"I thought department stores had all the Christmas stuff settled in June," Dad was saying.

"Normally, they do," Mom said, turning on the TV. "But as I've said, this Greymer store was in a mess. The ex-manager was incompetent. The store has never had a Santa before!"

"No Santa?" Dad raised a bushy eyebrow. "Poor rich suburban brats."

Why'd he say that? After all, we're in suburbia and we're not rich. Well-off because of mom's fabulous job and once dad gets his cartooning career in full gear—*hey!* Maybe I won't have to worry about future employment. I'll be an heiress!

"Last year, I arrived too late to notice that there wasn't a store Santa. This year, there'll be one and everyone will know it was *my* idea. It's a marvelous one, isn't it, Sarah?"

"Guess so."

"Well, I think it's a terrific idea!" Mom said loudly, flipping channels. "And if the powers that be agree—my bosses in the city—I'll get a fat bonus."

"Yeah, then it's good," I said and added quickly before mom had a chance to say anything else (she's awfully carried away with her job lately), "What are you watching?"

"*The Awful Truth.* It's a—"

"Don't tell me! A Cary Grant film!"

Mom laughed. "You got me. I've seen it twelve times."

"I'm getting more ice cream," I said. A Cary Grant film means mom is glued to the set, reciting the dialogue, while dad sketches and sings along with all the record commercials. Not my idea of a wonderful Friday night.

After getting another heaping bowl of ice cream, I leafed

through the newspaper and checked the hockey schedules. The Rangers were playing Hartford and the game was on the radio. Eating chocolate ice cream, listening to an exciting hockey game, staring at my pictures of Jim Craig, and playing with Sir L was my idea of a wonderful Friday night.

The next day, a cold, horrible rain beat down.

"I cancel my appointment, right?"

Dad shook his head. "Wrong. I'll drive you."

"I'd rather walk."

He looked hurt but I couldn't help it. Dad curses when he drives and when the weather's this rotten, I'd feel like I was in the middle of an R-rated film.

"Aren't you leery about going to the dentist by yourself?" he asked, walking me to the door.

"No, should I be?" Dad always has to be escorted to the dentist. "Besides, I'll stop by Connie's and ask if she wants to tag along."

"Have enough money?"

He wasn't asking about the bill; that was sent to the house. "Well . . ."

He gave me several dollars and I thanked him. No way can I go into the village without getting something to eat. Connie never has any money for food; she spends her allowance on audio equipment and "violent hockey games."

As soon as I rang Connie's doorbell, her little brother, Jimmy, hollered, "I got it! I got it!" And Mrs. Russo yelled, "Ask who's there first!" The Russos migrated from New York City, too. Old habits are hard to break.

"Who is it?" Jimmy screamed.

"What's it," I answered.

The door flung open and he jumped up and down. "You're it!"

We always go through that routine; little kids are funny.

"Hello, Sarah!" Mrs. Russo said. "Get out of that miserable rain. Connie's in the kitchen. Where else?"

I put my umbrella in the rack and trotted into the pine-paneled kitchen. "Julia Child rides again," I said.

"Hi, Sarah. Found the greatest recipe for butterscotch squares."

"That's nice. I was going to ask you to come to the dentist with me but I see you're busy." I pointed to the brown and orange mess in a metal mixing bowl.

"Stop by when you're through."

I started to say okay because that concoction would turn into something delectable but a deep voice interrupted.

"If it isn't the girl goalie!"

"Why don't you find a zipper large enough for your mouth, Tony?" Connie hollered.

I didn't say boo. Tony's in high school, a sarcastic creep and a male chauvinist pig. But I'd never tell him so to his face. He's also mean.

"At Memorial High we don't allow girls on the hockey team."

"And Memorial hasn't had a winning record in its history," Connie said.

Connie may believe my hockey life can get me killed (or detoothed) but she's on my side about my right to play.

"I'm going to the dentist," I said hurriedly. Tony was giving his sister a horrible glare. I didn't want any trouble. "See you around, Julia Child!" I said to Connie.

By the time I arrived at Dr. Marangi's office, I was soaked; my umbrella had turned inside out. I sat across from a girl who looked about my age. She was reading a tattered copy of *Cosmo*; she looked at me and gave a superior smirk. I felt like I'd walked into the fourth dimension. Or maybe there was dog doo on my shoe. I hadn't and there wasn't. But it sure felt that way.

I picked up a copy of *Sports Illustrated* and thumbed through it. It was filled with college football. Now, that's a game you can get hurt playing! When I finished reading about USC's fantastic team, I thought about Tony Russo (he plays football). No girls on the hockey squad. Wait until Piggy enrolls next September! I was having a terrific daydream about Tony and Piggy's first encounter when the nurse announced that I was next.

I put the magazine down and entered Dr. Marangi's antiseptic office. My dentist is short, bald except for two long strands of gray hair that drape his forehead, and he has a soft, teeny-weeny voice which makes me think of Bashful.

"Good morning, Sarah! Time for our annual checkup."

"You, too?" I said, hopping into *the* chair. He knows I hate "our" and "we."

"All right," he conceded. "*Your* checkup." He clanked dangerous-looking instruments on that round, swing counter attached to the drill. He tied a bib around my neck and my stomach growled. When you're in a crowd, you can pretend it's someone else's tummy but when there's only you and someone else, you can't fake it. I tried to melt into the leather chair. He yanked me up again.

"Open wide."

I did and felt like a zoo specimen. He kept saying, "Mmmmm . . ." "Uhhh . . ." and "I see." Finally he stopped. "Are you still playing hockey, Sarah?"

"Yes," I said, wiggling my tongue. Keeping my mouth open like that makes me terribly dry.

"Amazing."

"What's amazing?"

"The fact that you still have your teeth."

3

Afterwards, I walked through the rainy village and for some reason, I was depressed. Usually, Tony's put-downs don't get to me. Neither does Dr. Marangi's concern about my teeth. After all, it *is* his job! But this morning, both got to me. My weirdness became stronger by the hour.

The library stood in front of me. Once inside, I stopped at the bulletin board. Kittens for sale. A meeting of the historical society. A notice for the Topsy-Turvy Dance. That's a girl-ask-boy thing. I'd considered asking Alex but the next morning is the Tornado game and well, I want to rest up for my big chance.

"Hi, Sarah!"

I turned around. There, with an armful of thick, maroon-covered books, was David Underwood, Gayle's friend.

"Going to the dance?" he asked, looking up. Height isn't David's strong point.

"No. Are you going with Gayle?"

He shook his head. "She didn't ask me. Barbara Brewer did so I'm going with her. Uh, Sarah," David said, looking terribly shy behind his big eyeglasses. "Do you know what's wrong with Gayle? Uh . . ."

"She's *uh* with me, too. I thought she was upset because of a fight with you."

"No."

I shrugged.

David sighed. "If she hasn't told you what's wrong, I guess she hasn't told anyone. I better check these out." He thumped the books. "I'm doing an article for the newspaper. See you in school."

I was more curious about Gayle's problem now. I debated whether to stop at her house but her mother gives piano lessons on Saturdays and I didn't want to interrupt. Mrs. Steinberg is a wild-woman when she's teaching. The thought of tasting Connie's orange and brown mess appealed to me but another insult bout with Tony didn't.

"Home, feet!"

"You had a phone call," Dad said when I walked in. "Steve Hollaway."

I was surprised. Must be a change in practice.

I got out the telephone book and looked up Hollaway. *Hollaway Optical.* Wondered if the owners were any relation to Steve? I continued down the listing. *Steven G. Hollaway, Sr.* Never heard anyone call Steve Junior. He doesn't look like a junior anybody. He stands a head taller than everyone else. 1500 *Newman Lane*. Hey, that's the part of town where all the "old, old money" houses are. Even older than the Steinbergs. Steve never struck me as rich, either.

"Hello, may I speak to Steve, please? This is Sarah Dunes." I always volunteer everything. Parents just ask for it if you don't.

"Is there a change in the practice sked?" I asked when Steve got on.

"Huh?" He laughed. "No, it's still Monday afternoon. That's the only time we can get the rink."

"Yeah, that's lousy. Why do we have to buy rink time? Too bad the school doesn't have extra funds so we could build our own . . ." I swallowed my last words. After all, Steve didn't want to know my financial opinions. I waited for him to speak.

"You know the Topsy-Turvy Dance? The girl-ask-boy one? Sarah, Piggy asked me!"

I think I howled because Steve said I'd broken the sound barrier, not to mention his eardrums. "What—what did you say when she did?"

"I told her I was already asked."

"Good for you. That's that then," I said, wondering what all the excitement was about and wondering why Steve had called . . .

"She asked me with who—"

"She would!"

"And the truth is I didn't really have a date so I said the first name I could think of. I said you, Sarah."

I dropped the phone.

"Sarah! Sarah!"

I picked it up again. "Me?" I squeaked.

"Yeah. Look, if you've already asked someone else, I'll understand."

"Steve, I was going to rest up for the Tornado game. I figure that's my big chance, you know."

"Then you didn't ask anyone else?"

I blew air into my cheeks and made myself look like a chipmunk. "No. Okay, I'll go with you."

"Steve asked me to the Topsy-Turvy," I told dad when I got off the phone.

"You don't sound too thrilled. Is Steve two-headed? Or maybe that goalie mask he wears during the game really isn't a mask and he really looks like that. Or . . ."

"*Whoa!*" I shouted. Dad can go on for hours with the "Or" game. I filled him in.

"Oh, you're helping out a friend then. I'm sure you'll have a good time."

"Yeah." But I wasn't at all sure.

Sunday morning was a lazy, semirainy, semicloudy day and I wanted nothing more than to remain in bed until noon. I listened to my favorite rock station; the disc jockey announced a "Golden Oldie" and played the Beach Boys song, "Help Me, Rhonda." I remembered my aunt's visit so I got out of bed and got dressed.

Mom was in the kitchen, yanking items from the cabinets, and dad was struggling with a bow tie. He has an absolute *thing* about bow ties. He wasn't dressing up for Rhonda's visit; Sunday's the busiest day for a realtor, even a part-time one. Lots of people from the city look at houses on Sundays. He's already made one commission this month.

"Tell me what the Giants do," he said, running out the back door.

"They'll lose," I said with confidence. "What are you making?" I asked mom.

"Thought I'd try—"

The doorbell rang. I ran to answer it. It was my aunt, looking as only Rhonda can look. She's tall and skinny and *gorgeous!* She wore a beautiful black leather trench coat and a floppy red hat.

"Sarah, you've grown another inch!"

"Only one-quarter," I said, giving her a hug.

"Whatever. I saw Win sneaking off into the woods."

"He happens to have a client," Mom said. She was standing in the hallway, spatula in hand.

"Really?" Rhonda laughed. Rhonda and dad don't see eye-to-eye. He probably was sneaking off to avoid her. "I'm so glad to be here! The city's *dreadful* on Sunday!"

"I thought it was *dreadful* all the time. That's why we moved out."

"I thought it was because of your job, Roxanne."

"I could have commuted."

Oh, boy! It's going to be one of *those* visits! Makes me glad I don't have any brothers or sisters. Mom isn't sarcastic with Aunt Rosiland. Maybe that's because she's older or because we don't see her that often—I play the "Or" game a lot, too.

Rhonda took off her coat. Underneath, she had on a sleek yellow jump suit. She looked like she should be shot out of a cannon.

"A slave to the stove, eh Roxanne?"

I followed them into the kitchen.

"Not really. This is the first time I've prepared dinner all week. I'm using the manicotti recipe Connie gave you, Sarah."

"Oh, no!" Rhonda groaned. "At your age, girls shouldn't be tying themselves down to housework! They'll never be able to break the habit!" She snapped her orange fingernails. "Know what? This 'housewife' girl should meet the other one."

"Huh?" Mom and I asked in unison.

"This domesticated girl should meet your friend who wants to be the next Barbara Walters."

"They know each other intimately," I said. "Connie's both people."

"Oh," Rhonda said. She sounded disappointed.

"Everyone should know how to cook," Mom said, stuffing a manicotti tube. *"Everyone."*

"I will. When I get older."

Mom laughed. "I didn't mean you, Sarah. My remark was directed toward Rhonda."

"Ugh! Why should I cook when there are a zillion restaurants in Manhattan?"

"Because you don't have a zillion dollars, that's why. Unless they've increased unemployment benefits recently."

Mom bent over to check the oven. Rhonda pretended to kick her in the rear. I giggled; mom wanted to know what was so hilarious. We didn't tell her.

"Didn't you have a game yesterday?" Rhonda asked.

"Yeah." Here it comes.

"How many shots did you stop?"

"None. I didn't play."

"I knew it!" Rhonda said triumphantly. "They're discriminating against you. They let you on the team as a token gesture. Roxanne, why don't you speak to Sarah's coach?"

"Sarah, tell my sister who scored the hat trick for the Dolphins."

"Piggy Barnes. *She's* our best forward."

For a moment, Rhonda's beautiful face clouded. Then she brightened. "All right. Piggy Barnes will be the best forward in the NHL someday and Sarah will be the premiere goalie!"

She smiled at me and I couldn't help but notice her teeth are like little pearls. Mine are just there. *There.* For which I suppose I should be grateful. Connie and Dr. Marangi were getting to me.

I decided to change the subject. "I'm going to the Topsy-Turvy Dance after all."

"Fantastic!" Rhonda said, walking over to the fridge. She removed a jar of stuffed olives, opened the jar, and groped for a handful. "But Sarah, I hope you didn't go the safe route and ask that Alex boy again. You do have to play the field, you know!"

If you look like Rhonda, that's simple. If you look like me, it's a Herculean task. "No. I'm going with Steve Hollaway. He's the first-string goalie."

Rhonda pulled the pimiento out of an olive. "Not bad strategy. Not bad at all. He'll get so tired from dancing that you'll have to start the next game."

"One, we're playing the Tornadoes the next day and they're a terrible team. I *know* I'll play against them. Two, if he gets tired from dancing, obviously, so will I, and three, I'm not using any dumb strategy! Steve asked me—"

"He asked you?" Rhonda's neatly plucked eyebrow jumped. "But isn't it a girl-ask-boy—"

"Rhonda," Mom said, not taking her eyes off Connie's

neatly printed recipe card. "Eat another olive. In fact, eat the whole jar."

Thanks, Mom, I said to myself. Rhonda's visits are usually fun, even if we do argue about me and the team. But today, like yesterday and a whole lot of recent days, nothing was fun. I even wished she'd devour the whole jar, which was a rotten thing to wish for, since too many olives give Rhonda the runs.

"It's time for kickoff!" I said and dashed into the living room before anyone could stop me.

What a lousy weekend! What was happening to me? Maybe my astrological signs are in conflict or a witch has cast a spell on me. But I don't understand astrology and I don't know any witches. I hoped the Giants would surprise me and win. That'd cheer me up!

They lost, 53–6.

4

When we lived in the city, I rode a bus to school. Not a school bus but an ordinary city one, which crawled with roaches, litter, and was covered with graffiti. When we moved up here, I looked forward to riding on a bright, orange school bus, sitting with my best friend and doing last minute homework.

As it turned out, I lived three blocks from Larimer Junior High.

I meet Gayle on the corner. Connie goes to Immaculate Conception School; she gets to travel on a school bus and she says there are roaches, litter, and graffiti on it so I guess I'm not missing anything.

After my rotten Sunday, I wasn't enthused about seeing Gayle—not with the way she'd been acting lately. But as soon as I said hi, I knew her mood had changed. She wore her favorite orange and gray angora scarf with matching mittens. She looked like a model in the Sears catalog.

"How was your weekend, Sarah? I'm really sorry I couldn't go to the dentist with you."

"That's okay. I had a miserable weekend."

She wrinkled her tiny nose. "What went wrong?"

I filled her in on Rhonda.

"Yecch!"

"And that wasn't the half of it. When we were eating dinner, she carried on about not being able to find work. Dad suggested part-time employment and mom offered to put in a word for her at the Manhattan Greymer & Greymer."

"I take it she didn't go for the idea."

"She almost went for their heads! She started yelling about how she'd studied to be an engineer and how settling for less just wouldn't be right. Then mom said what about the money she was accepting from the government . . ."

Gayle giggled. "Bet she loved that!"

I rolled my eyes. "Then Rhonda argued that women are constantly expected to take less money and dad countered with, 'Unemployment benefits are the same for everyone. Have some more olives, Rhonda.' " I did my best to imitate dad's deep voice.

Gayle cracked up; she knows about Rhonda's olive problem.

"She left right after dinner. Mom and dad argued about her all evening. Not exactly argued," I added. "They agreed about her but yet they, uh . . . argued." I shook my head. "You know how parents are. Hey, here I am going on and on and you haven't said a thing about your weekend."

"Mine was super! My parents took me out to dinner at Wo Luck's—"

"You had two shrimp toasts, right?"

"Three! Then yesterday, we spent the whole day singing around the piano and playing Scrabble."

That didn't sound like a *super* weekend to me but Gayle sure seemed pleased about it. I was dying to ask what had been bothering her but she'd tell me when she was ready.

"How about the *DQ* after school? My treat."

"Yummy!" I smacked my lips. "But I can't make it. Practice."

"I forgot. You have the Tornado game coming up."

"That's not all. You're not going to believe this but Piggy asked Steve to the Topsy-Turvy and he nearly had a coronary so he said he was going with me! Which means, I'm not going to rest up for the game as I'd planned."

"Incredible! But a dance is much more fun than resting, Sarah."

"Maybe. Um, I saw David."

She waved a mittened hand. "He's been asked by Barbara. I called him last night and found out."

We were now one block from school and had slowed our pace considerably.

"Will you ask someone else? Any boy will say yes, you gotta know that!"

"Thanks! I asked Ralph; he's in my art class."

I didn't know the kids in her art class. Gayle's in there seventh period while I'm in sewing. She's talented. Later this season, she's going to paint blue dolphins on my mask.

We were now across the street from our five-day-a-week jail. I looked at Gayle. She shrugged. No getting out of it! We marched into the masses.

My day went okay. *At first*. My English book report was returned to me. C+. There was also a note from Mrs. Jacobs. *"Good thing these classics have been made into films. However, Hollywood is notorious for changes in plot line."* Which explained why the movie was so short and the book so thick (and covered in a nubby, worn out, hunter green jacket). I liked seventh grade required reading a lot better; those books were thinner and there were a batch of sports books to choose from.

As I said, the beginning of the day was okay. I answered two questions right in math and there was vanilla pudding in the cafeteria.

Then came sewing. Miss Mitchum teaches the course. The first day of school, she stood in front of the room, cleared her throat twice, patted her purple beehive hairdo and said, "I am *Miss* Mitchum. Never *Miz*." Naturally, everyone calls her Miz.

Anyway, I get along with her. Why? Because I'm good in sewing. It's one of my hobbies. Since most of the kids are sloppy and disinterested, the teacher likes me.

Or did until today.

Our latest project was a workshirt. She tried to get us to

do blouses and shirts. She doesn't approve of boys in sewing. The fact that, outside of my stuff, Alex's is the best in the class, doesn't thrill her. But back to the workshirts. The class argued that blouses *and* shirts would involve more than one pattern and she'd end up teaching two projects instead of one and that would get confusing for everyone. Besides, one project for girls and one for boys was sexist. When Alex said that, she gave in.

My shirt's pale gray with skinny mauve lines running vertically. I'd cut the pattern and Miss Mitchum was oohing and ahhing over it.

"What a wonderful seamstress you'll make, Sarah Dunes!"

"Really?" Everyone thinks I'll make a wonderful something-or-other. Nice to know *they* have all this confidence in me.

"It's reassuring to see girls following the more genteel tasks in life once again."

That's when Steve opened the door.

"Yes?" she said. "What do you want, young man?"

He walked over to my table and handed her a folded piece of paper. She read it quickly and shook her head.

"That's the problem with school sports. They take precedence over everything else. *Alex Smythe!*" she hollered. "Go with this young man. You have hockey practice."

The class howled; Alex gets knocked down in Ping-Pong.

"Um, that's for me." I stood up and folded my shirt. "I'm the hockey player."

"*Sarah Dunes! You?*" She frowned. "Sit."

I stared down at Miss Mitchum. "What?" I squeaked.

"You heard me! Sit. Young man, I will not have my class disrupted in this manner. Sarah Dunes may join your practice session after my class. Not during it."

"*Miz* Mitchum," Steve said softly. "We rent out rinks. The Blue Dolphins have ice time now. We need Sarah."

"*No!*"

I blinked and felt my face growing a deep shade of magenta. How could she do this? There were maybe fifteen minutes left in the period.

"Miss Mitchum, I really have to go," I said.

"Sit down, Sarah Dunes!"

She didn't add, "Weird Person," but it was in her tone.

"I'll get Coach Caplan," Steve said. "Don't worry, Sarah."

For the first time since the third grade when a boy ate my science project, I wanted to cry in school. I gulped twice and took a deep breath and choked on the teacher's hair spray.

"I'm astonished at you, Sarah Dunes. Hockey is a violent sport. Disgusting for a girl to play!" And she strode away.

I glanced around the classroom. All eyes were on me so I figured to meet them full on. Staring back was also a good way to keep from crying. One by one, the kids turned away. Except for Alex. He winked and slipped me a note. *"Don't worry,"* he'd written. *"I fought to get into this class and won. You can fight to get out."*

I managed a weak smile. But I didn't want a battle! What was all the fuss about? More to the point—*why me?*

The door opened again. Coach Caplan appeared, stick in hand. She's going to clobber Miss Mitchum! But she ignored the sewing teacher and ambled over to me.

"Here's your stick, Sarah. C'mon, we'll be late for practice."

"You're disrupting my class!" Miss Mitchum screeched.

"Sarah Dunes happens to be a member of my hockey team. There is a practice, which is costing us money. If you have any argument on the subject, I suggest you take it up with Mr. Phelps, our illustrious principal. I'm sure he'll set you straight. After all, his *daughter* covers the Buffalo Sabres for an Erie County newspaper."

Miss Mitchum sputtered and threw her hands up, hitting her purple beehive. The hairdo shook . . . then tumbled down her face . . . then her throat and finally onto the floor . . . leaving her practically bald.

Coach Caplan and I exited from the room and ran downstairs. "I don't know who I feel more sorry for," I said. "Her, for losing her purple nest or me, for the way she'll treat me tomorrow."

"Don't give it another thought, Sarah," Coach Caplan

said, bounding into the parking lot. "If she does give you a hard time, we'll take it to Mr. Phelps."

More commotion! The one thing I didn't need. I made up my mind. No matter how nasty Miss Mitchum became, I'd keep mum.

I hopped into Coach Caplan's yellow Camaro. Steve, Piggy, and the others on her line were jammed into the car. Piggy's presence made a good ad for using underarm deodorant.

"Open a window!" Coach Caplan said, obviously agreeing with my unspoken thoughts.

A window became all of them and the car became cold. I looked at the heavy and menacing clouds. Snow or rain? Didn't matter. With the way this day was going, I figured a monsoon was in order.

"Get some serious work in," Mr. Darrow said to me when we arrived at the rink. "You'll probably play against the Tornadoes."

"Yeah, we'll have a seven or eight goal lead at the end of the first period," Russ Gruber said; he's on Piggy's line.

"Even you should be able to make that stand up," Piggy said. She clamped on her helmet, spit on the ice, and skated away.

Coach Caplan patted my arm. "Remember, you're a stand-up goalie. You challenge the shooters. Steve has a tendency to go down too soon. The opposition knows that and they often score on him when he's down."

I didn't remind her Steve's goals-against-average was a mere 2.10. She'd only counter with, "But your goals-against is zero, Sarah!" Which is absolutely true—however, I haven't played yet.

I slipped on my mask and made my own groove in front of the nets. After brushing away ice chips with my stick, I told them I was ready.

The team practiced shots from the point. When Piggy wound up, I winced inwardly, but her two shots were wide of the cage by five feet. Stopping Russ' huge slap shot gained me a round of applause. I bowed.

Mr. Darrow blew his whistle. "Enough of that. Let's have some one-on-ones. That's like a breakaway, Sarah."

He always redefines terms to me. He doesn't say much but I don't think he's happy about two girls on the team.

However, I was happy about the one-on-one confrontations. They're my favorites; Coach Caplan is right about my stand-up methods. I never go down until the last possible instant. Only a super deke beats me. "Let's go!" I hollered.

Everything went according to plan. I stopped three shooters point blank. Then Piggy picked up the puck at the red line. She came straight down the ice. As usual, I stood my ground. Stood it until I noticed she wasn't slowing down as she approached the net. *Either shoot or deke, Piggy! You're skating too fast. Can't you see that?*

"Augggghhhhh!"

Piggy had barrelled into me. I don't know if I hit my shoulder on the goalpost first or slid down, hit my shoulder on Piggy's helmet, and then hit the post. All I knew was there were skates all around me and I was afraid to breathe.

"Why didn't you stop?" Coach Caplan's voice was loud and angry.

"Ah, I was tryin' this new play," Piggy retorted.

Mr. Darrow's voice was soft. "Can you move, Sarah?"

"I—I think so."

"You didn't hit your head, did you?"

Before I could reply, Coach Caplan pushed smelling salts under my nose and I gagged. She removed my mask. "How many fingers do I have, Sarah?"

"Five."

"Very funny. In front of your eyes." She wiggled her hand.

"Three."

"Good! Good!"

She *always* holds up three fingers when someone gets injured. But I really could see okay. I felt so pleased about that that I tried to move. I was no longer pleased. *"Oooww! My shoulder!"*

"We'll get you to a hospital. C'mon, boys, help the lady up."

I didn't protest. All I could think of was Piggy driving

down the ice. She'd charged me deliberately. That was the only explanation. *But why?*

Several boys carried me off, basket-style. If I hadn't been in pain, I would've been embarrassed. A goalie's equipment isn't lightweight.

"I'll call your mother," Steve said; he was one of the carriers.

"She's working. My dad's home."

They slid me into the Camaro. "Thanks, Steve," I said. *Steve.*

Piggy Barnes had asked Steve to the Topsy-Turvy; he refused. "I'm going with Sarah Dunes."

Piggy Barnes had flattened Sarah Dunes.

The monsoon had arrived.

5

"I'm sorry I had to work late tonight. Are you sure you're okay?" Mom asked, kissing my forehead.

"The doctor in the emergency room says my shoulder will be stiff for a couple of days but that's it," I said from my comfortable perch on the bed.

It was nearly nine o'clock, six hours after my accident. I felt okay; dad gave me three hot dogs drenched in mustard and smothered with sauerkraut for dinner. And I had mom and dad's little TV at the foot of my bed (once upon a time, I had one of my own but they took it away when they caught me watching "Outer Limits" reruns at 3:00 A.M.).

"Your father said you were fine, but my God! You scared me half-to-death, Sarah. I think you're going through an awkward stage."

"No, Piggy Barnes is."

"What?"

I gave mom my thoughts on what had happened.

She cursed vividly. "What some kids won't do to get what they want."

"But she hasn't gotten what she wants."

"Meaning?"

"I'm still okay to go to the Topsy-Turvy." Even if I wasn't sure going was the brightest move in the world.

"Sarah, you're something!" Mom kissed me again and messed my already messy hair. "You don't have to go to school tomorrow."

Dad popped his head in the doorway. "How's 'my kid'?"

We giggled. Mom demanded to know what was so funny.

Dad explained, "After Steve called, I rushed over to the emergency room. Grabbed the first nurse I saw—"

"Winston! Grabbing nurses!" Mom teased.

Dad stuck his tongue out and continued, "I told her, 'my kid,' had been injured in a hockey scrimmage. She smiled a smile that rivals the Mona Lisa and told me to follow her. So, I went over to this cubicle and there was 'my kid.' Some seven-year-old boy with a bloody nose!"

"Serves you right!" Mom laughed. "You should have said daughter."

"The nurse got very huffy when I set her straight. 'We should not allow young girls to play violent games!' "

"I heard the phone ring a zillion times."

"My, what big ears you have, Sarah," Dad said. "I turned the bell off on your extension so you wouldn't be disturbed."

"Who called?"

He put his thumb on his chin. "Coach Caplan, Mr. Darrow, Gayle, Connie, and Steve. I assured them you're alive and well." He posted himself in front of my phone. "Phone calls can wait. Dr. Underwood says you're to rest."

He shut the TV off and mom fluffed up the strawberry-colored quilt. They kissed me good-night and before they closed the door, Sir Lancelot's mewing became apparent. The bed depressed and his whiskers tickled my nose. "Thanks for coming here," I said. He mewed again.

The next morning my shoulder ached. Not bad but just enough to know my shoulder was different from the rest of my anatomy. I stood in front of my full-length mirror and rubbed on some awful-smelling ointment. Sir L sniffed, arched his back, and whizzed out of the room. "Fair weather friend!" I shouted after him. Not that I blamed him. The ointment really did stink. I went into the bathroom and threw talcum powder everywhere the ointment wasn't. After I stopped coughing, I walked downstairs.

Mom had already left for work but dad was on the kitchen phone. I put the kettle on so I'd have water for my instant cocoa and sat on the table.

"Yes, yes. I think that would be possible. Mmm . . ."

I frowned; it isn't easy to eavesdrop on dad's conversations. He uses cryptic sentences and nods a lot.

"Yes, sounds fair. I'll be over at two to sign."

"You sold the house you showed Sunday!" I said when he hung up.

"No. Sarah, why are there white footprints on the floor?"

I looked down and across the room. There was more talc on the house then on me by now.

"I'll clean it up before I go," Dad said absently.

"Go where?"

"Oh, Mr. Jennings, he's the one I showed the property to, he didn't like the house, but he did like my sketches."

Dad sketches everything he has to show to prospective clients. Says it makes the job tolerable.

"You sold the drawings of the property?"

"No, Mr. Jennings wants me to design his firm's Christmas cards," Dad said, pouring boiling water into my big Snoopy mug.

"That's terrific! But, um, isn't it a little late in the season?"

"Yeah, but his regular designer died and Mr. Jennings hadn't found anyone until he found me. He owns the Veronique Boutique."

My eyes bulged, Peter Lorre style (mom isn't the only one who's addicted to old movies). Veronique Boutique is in the village, around the corner from Dr. Marangi's office. The clothes sold in the shop are expensive, just like those in the Riviera Wing of Greymer & Greymer. In fact,

45

Veronique Boutique is mom's biggest competitor.

"Dad, don't you realize—"

"Of course I do! If Jennings is pleased with my cards, I'll get more assignments from him. Super, huh?"

With dad's skinny face all aglow, I didn't have the heart to tell him he was about to enter the enemy camp.

After cocoa, I napped. When I woke up, dad had left for his appointment. I stayed glued to the soap operas. They were really exciting today, with two marriages on the rocks, an affair beginning, and the wrap-up of a murder trial. The doorbell rang. I peeked out my bedroom window. Connie and Gayle stood at the front door. I yelled and tossed down my key (I didn't feel like going downstairs). A minute later, they were in my room.

"Are you okay?" Connie demanded, flopping on the floor. "Everyone's yakking about what happened. The news even traveled to I Commit Suicide."

I Commit Suicide is the student translation of Immaculate Conception School.

"By the time the story got to us, I figured you were near dead or at the least confined to a wheelchair. You smell funny but you look okay." Connie pushed her hair behind her ears. "You really scared us, Sarah, didn't she, Gayle?"

"Yeah, but she's fine."

Connie whispered, "Is it true Piggy Barnes was stoned and didn't know what she was doing?"

"Not really." I gave them the whole story.

Gayle shook her head. "That's too much! All because a boy turned her down!"

"Well, you don't know what rejection feels like, Gayle Steinberg! You're the prettiest girl in your class!"

Gayle blushed; I jumped in. "Listen, plenty of people get turned down without trying to maim someone else. Piggy is a mental case."

"But you're still going to the dance, right?" Connie asked; I nodded. "Wow! Promise to call me the minute you get home! Better yet, come over! My father will pick you and Gayle up after the dance. Or Tony."

I choked on the last statement.

"Okay, no Tony, but you two have to tell me *everything* that happens!"

Connie is crazy on the subject of boys and going to dances and stuff like that. Her parents won't let her go to dances or on dates until next year when she's officially in high school.

They stayed awhile longer. I saw them to the door; dad was coming up the walk, arms filled with brown bags. The aroma of *moo goo gai pan* drifted to me. When he was inside the house, I also spotted a bottle of champagne. He probably planned to celebrate his new job—I wondered how mom would feel toasting the competition.

"I stopped by Greymer," Dad said. "Your mom's working late again."

He missed her being home. So did I but I guess it wasn't

the same way. I'd made friends since we moved here but dad kept pretty much to himself. Most of the neighborhood men commuted to the city and played racquetball or golf on the weekends. Dad usually worked on the weekends. Mom is dad's best friend. I let him have extra mushrooms; he loves mushrooms.

"How's your shoulder?"

"The pain is going away. Just hope it's *all* gone by the weekend."

"Aha! For the dance!"

I made a goofy face. "No way! The Tornado game is my main concern." Why was everyone harping on the dance? I knew the answer. A dance was normal. A girl goalie wasn't. Sarah Dunes, Weird Person strikes again!

That night, the TV was filled with great programs. I was in the middle of conning dad into an extra show when the door opened. Mom strode in, two Greymer shopping bags in tow.

"About time," Dad muttered. Then in a louder, friendlier voice, he said, "Want some Chinese food? I can heat it up for you."

Mom grimaced; she hates takeout. She enjoys her own Cantonese specialties. So do I—when she gets around to preparing them.

"What's in here?" I poked my nose into a bag filled with green-and-white foil-wrapped packages.

"None of your beeswax," she replied, which meant Christmas presents. "Except for this." From the other bag, she handed me an unwrapped white box. "Open it."

"Whee!" I ripped off the cover. Inside was a pale gray skirt and a dark green pullover. Real wool, too. "Fantastic!"

"I didn't think your red-and-orange dress fit anymore and I doubt if your hockey uniform is suitable for a dance."

I didn't mind her saying that. I love new clothes. "Thanks! I'll try it on right after the show."

"Show? What show?"

"The terrific one that's on next."

"Good night, Sarah," Mom said sweetly but firmly.

"Night," I mumbled. I gave in so easily because their portable was still at the foot of my bed.

En route to school the next day, Gayle invited me over to her house Monday afternoon. "If there's no hockey practice," she added.

"There isn't. I don't think so anyway. Sounds great."

"I'll invite Connie, too."

"Great," I repeated. The Steinbergs give us full run of the house, which means raiding the refrigerator, playing the pinball machines in the basement, listening to cassettes, all without anyone telling us to keep it down.

At school, everyone asked how I was. The attention was nice and I *should've* appreciated it more but after the way things had been happening to me lately, I kind of wished everyone would ignore me.

The shoulder problem eased up and I even practiced on

roller skates (we couldn't rent out ice time anymore this week) in front of my house, pretending the mailbox was my goal cage. I also had to hold on to it several times to avoid falling. Waverly has to be the bumpiest street in the world!

Saturday meant two things. An appointment with Dr. Marangi and the dance. I really wasn't looking forward to either.

Dr. Marangi opened our session with, "I hear we had a slight mishap this week."

"You, too? No kidding!"

"All right, Sarah. *You* had an accident."

I'll break him of that habit yet. "Yeah, I bruised my shoulder," I said, eyeing him as he filled a hypo with no-vocaine. I don't mind the actual shot. However, watching him prepare it made me want to crawl through the radiator pipes.

"At least it wasn't your teeth, Sarah."

"Oh, wow! Guess I'm just plain lucky, huh?" I snapped.

He whirled around; I sunk into the chair. Even though he insists on *we*, Dr. Marangi is one of my favorite adults. I mumbled an apology. It's his job to worry about my teeth, I reminded myself. He doesn't mean anything by it.

Even after I left the office, the whole left side of my face remained numb. I touched my nose to make sure it wasn't running.

"Picking your nose, Female Jock?"

Tony Russo was leaning against the window of the pizza parlor. I wanted to reply but the extra pieces of silver filling were swimming through my mouth. Hated to swallow that junk.

"My sister says you're going to a dance tonight."

I decided I didn't want to speak to him so I tried to walk past but he blocked my path. As small as Connie is, that's how big her brother is. He sneered. "Enjoy it while you can, Female Jock."

"Huh?" I mumbled. Even that small word caused silver tidbits to slide down my dry throat. *Please no, I'll gag!*

"Maybe being a dumb Female Jock in junior high is okay with your silly friends but lemme tell ya, Sarah Dune Buggy, older guys hate dumb jock broads." He smiled and moved out of my way. "Like I said, enjoy the dance while you can. No way you'll ever go to another one."

I gagged on the silver junk.

6

There's a trick to making novocaine wear off faster. Keep moving your mouth and cheeks. Dad said he couldn't tell if I was doing isometrics or trying out for a part in a monster movie.

The pins and needles feeling subsided but Tony's remarks hung with me. How could a super person like Connie have a creep like him for a brother? And it didn't seem possible Mr. and Mrs. Russo had produced Tony, either. Maybe he's a test tube baby? *Test Tube Tony.* That's what I'd call him from now on—not to his face, of course.

As I filled the tub with hot water, the phone rang. It was Connie. "Are you all excited? What are you going to wear?"

"Not really and mom bought me a terrific skirt and sweater from the store."

"How can you not be excited? I am and I'm not even going! I'm also like a crazy person for another reason."

"Connie, what are you talking about?"

"Do you know what happens two weeks from now?"

"Yeah, a game with the Yellow Jackets. I'll never get to play against them."

"Sarah, I'm not talking about hockey!"

"I figured as much. So, what's your big news?"

"The test for St. Catherine's."

I whistled. St. Catherine's has its own radio station and special courses in media. It's also a tough school to get into. And Connie's like me—not the world's biggest brain.

"I'll cram and cram! And pray, too," she said. "Sarah, my parents were so disappointed when Tony had to go to public high school. He flunked the test for St. Andrew's. They're not going to let that happen again. They're going to make sure I study and study! Sarah, I have to get in!"

"Don't worry. You will." She needed a pep talk.

"Oh, I'm going to study and study! That's why I called now. I'll be real busy during the next two weeks. You won't mind not coming over or calling me after the dance?"

"Of course not! I have to rest up for my big day against the Tornadoes anyway."

"Good, I knew you'd understand. And tell Gayle I won't be able to make it Monday afternoon."

I heard a noise, peeked out in the hallway and nodded. "Listen, my dad's yelling about me causing the next flood. When can I call you?"

Connie said Tuesday after eight would be fine. "My parents go to bingo then."

"What do you mean you're not hungry?" Dad demanded awhile later.

I sat at the kitchen table, my yellow bathrobe tight around me. "I can't eat anything."

"Aha! You're nervous about the dance, aren't you? You *do* like Steve a little—"

I waved my hand. "My nervousness has nothing to do with him. Well, maybe it does, but not in the way you think. I'm afraid Piggy will brain me. Or drown me in the punch."

"Sarah, if Piggy got turned down by Steve, what makes you think she'll even show at the dance?"

"Mmm, hadn't thought of that. Thanks, Dad! Maybe I will have a small peanut butter and jelly sandwich." I had two large ones and three glasses of milk.

After I got dressed, I looked in the mirror, once, real quick-like, and turned away. Gayle spends hours in front of the mirror, putting on makeup and practicing being sexy. Connie makes believe the mirror is a TV monitor and she recites the news and worries if she's photogenic enough for the tube. Me, I know what I look like. My hair is short but nice and thick, my nose is too flat, and I look fifteen instead of thirteen. Once you know what you look like, mirrors don't help much.

"Fantastic!" Mom said, walking into my room. She had come home on time. "You look more like Rhonda everyday. I really wanted to see you off on this date."

"It's not my first," I reminded her. "I went out with Alex Smythe, remember?"

"Mmmm, but this date is much more intriguing. After all, he claims to have pulled your name out of thin air. Ever think why he did that, Sarah?"

Mom had a teasing glint in her eyes. It was the kind of glint she gets when Rhonda has boyfriend trouble. Luckily, the doorbell rang.

"Hi, Sarah," Steve said when I arrived downstairs. "Hi, Mr. Dunes, Mrs. Dunes. You look nice, Sarah."

"So do you," I said. Well, he did! He was wearing a bright red turtleneck which made his hair look more orange and he had on this great brown leather jacket.

I grabbed my coat and said bye to my folks. Trying to make conversation with grown-ups is difficult enough without having them inspect you like supermarket produce, which my parents had been doing to Steve and me.

"That's a neat house you have," he said once we were outside. "We live in an old one, too."

"Much older," I said, thinking about the homes on Newman.

"Yeah, I guess so," he said slowly. "Uh, we have a secret passageway. It's under the back stairs."

"Neat," I whistled.

Steve sighed. He seemed relieved that I thought so. However, he didn't say anything. We walked in silence until we reached Collier. Steve was real talkative on the ice and when I saw him at school. Why didn't he speak now? Probably because he's sorry he picked Sarah Dunes, Weird Person out of the air. I was awfully self-conscious but I also knew not talking for another two blocks would drive me batty.

"My folks said I could go to a hockey camp this summer."

As we walked under a streetlight, I saw Steve smile. "I went to one last summer. You can pick up some terrific pointers at them."

Then he got talkative! He ran down a list of ways a goalie can legally delay the game, trip people in the crease without the referee getting wise and generally cause chaos without receiving a penalty. By the time he stopped talking long enough to catch his breath, we were at the dance.

Gayle spotted us as soon as we walked through the doors. Her date, Ralph, was only her height but he didn't make any cracks about *my* height, which a lot of short boys do. He was even a hockey fan. Unfortunately, his favorite team was the Philadelphia Flyers.

"C'mon!"

Steve grabbed my hand and there I was—in the middle of the floor, with dozens of other kids who didn't know how to dance, either. I felt right at home. Steve wasn't bad. At least he didn't knock me on the floor the way Alex did at one party. That was particularly embarrassing since I landed on the hostess' toy poodle. It's hard to believe such harmless looking creatures have such sharp teeth! When I get my dog, it won't be a poodle.

"He's terrific!" Gayle squealed to me between dances.

We were by the water fountain. I wouldn't touch the punch. It looked like Hawaiian Punch with corn oil floating on top. The water was ice-cold and delicious.

"Ralph seems okay," I said, wiping my chin.

Gayle giggled. "Sarah! I meant Steve. You're lucky he lied to Piggy."

"Lucky?"

"Sure! If he didn't lie, you wouldn't be here. Isn't this more fun than sitting home?"

I didn't answer right away. *Was it more fun?* The gym was done up with flashing lights and rock music pounded from every corner. I'd danced nearly every number with Steve and one with Ralph. Because of all the dancing, my new wool sweater clung to me and my pantyhose had wrinkled at the ankles. If I were home, I'd be doing absolutely nothing except maybe watching TV and resting up for the Tornado game. *My game.*

"I'd rather be home."

"That's weird!"

So, Gayle agreed with my opinion of me. She'd never said it before. My mood, which had been none-too-happy to begin with, changed to unhappy. Not only would I rather be home, I actually resented Steve for lying to Piggy. And resented me for accepting instead of telling him to go jump in a lake. And . . . I was about to cry.

I scurried to the bathroom. After five minutes of reading graffiti in the stall, I was dry-eyed. When I walked out, the dance was breaking up.

"Thought I'd lost you," Steve said.

"No. Guess we'd better leave."

He agreed. Gayle tried to convince us to come over to her house. A whole group was going. Before Steve could accept (I think he wanted to), I jumped in. "We have a game tomorrow morning."

As he walked me home, I said, "I didn't see Piggy at the dance. At least I didn't notice her. Did you?"

"Who?"

"Piggy. Piggy Barnes. The other girl on the Dolphins? Our highest scorer? The one who asked you to the dance—"

"Right, right," he said hurriedly. "Guess she decided not to come."

Just like dad had suggested. Thank goodness! The evening had been a mess; she would've made it a catastrophe!

When we reached my house, two things struck me. One, would Steve want to come in? Two, would he kiss me good night? There's something about the star-goalie kissing the backup goalie that bothered me.

Steve settled both items. "Thanks, Sarah. I really had a great time. See you tomorrow." And he squeezed my arm and waved.

I wasn't sure if I was disappointed, relieved, hurt, insulted or what. But I returned the wave.

My parents were filled with questions. Dad was sketching and mom was planted in front of the set, watching *Holiday*, an ancient Cary Grant-Katherine Hepburn movie she's seen a hundred times. She asked her questions without taking her eyes off the screen.

I answered a couple of questions then tapped my foot. "I'm tired. It was just a silly dance. Steve is just another boy. Good night!"

I cried when I got to my room. The tears stopped when I remembered the Tornado game. I'd show them! *Show everyone!*

"It doesn't hurt! I swear my shoulder doesn't hurt!" I said to Coach Caplan in the locker room the next morning.

"Yecch! That's the worst colored bruise I've ever seen. Reminds me of the Hudson River."

"Well, the Hudson's still flowing and so am I."

"Yeah, even *you* oughta stop the Tornadoes."

Piggy rapped her stick on the floor. Never argue with Piggy, especially when she's armed. Besides, she's right about the Tornadoes. I will stop them; they're a joke. They went 0–15 last year and are 0–2 so far this season.

I skated once around the rink. Such a wonderful feeling to know I'd play today! Before hopping over the boards, I scanned the stands. Full house. No one I knew, though. Mom was too exhausted to get up at 8:00 A.M. on a Sunday morning to make a 9:30 hockey game and dad had morning clients. Connie had to study and Gayle hadn't mentioned anything about seeing the game. My moment of triumph alone. Oh, well, I couldn't let that bother me! I was much too excited about getting ice time! Second period, hurry up!

"The Star-Spangled Banner" was played and even before the scratchy recording finished, the crowd was screaming, "Go, Dolphins! Go Dolphs!"

As it turned out, that was all they had to cheer about.

Russ was flattened after the face-off and the Tornadoes' winger carried the puck into our zone. He shot and Steve went down too fast. Fifteen seconds into the first period and the lowly Tornadoes owned a one goal lead.

"You kids are taking them for granted!" Mr. Darrow thumped a towel on some handy helmets. "You can't do that! How many times have I got to tell you that!"

We managed a goal at the five-minute mark and I thought everything would be okay from here on in. That's when I looked at my stat sheet; the second-string goalie gets to keep a tally of shots-on-goal. The Tornadoes had nine already to two for us. Piggy had wound up several times from the point where she's usually deadly, but the shots went way wide all times. I didn't like the stats. The law of averages usually proves out. If they get enough shots, some of those shots will eventually take the right bounces and fall into the nets.

And two more did before the buzzer sounded. We were down 3–1 at the end of the first period.

Between periods, we all go to the same locker room. Mr. Darrow and Coach Caplan really gave it to us! Even though I'd done nothing more than watch and keep statistics, I felt as guilty and miserable as everyone else. Only my reason for the misery part was a little different than the rest of the team. If things kept up this way, I wouldn't get to play! And I'd been counting on this opportunity!

But there were two more periods to play. And two goals against such a rinky-dink club wouldn't be hard to make up. Once we tied it, there'd be no stopping us! And I'd get in during the third period. . . .

We didn't tie it. We lost the game 8–3 and I was the only Blue Dolphin not to participate.

I skipped the post-game meeting and walked home, still dressed in my uniform.

7

Don't Blame Sarah Dunes!

Sarah Dunes, a member of our Blue Dolphins hockey squad, cannot be faulted for yesterday's 8–3 debacle against the usually hapless Tornadoes.

Sarah cannot be faulted because Sarah is the backup goaltender and never got on the ice.

Lucky Sarah Dunes!

Those words of wisdom appeared on the first page of *Cross Words*, the student newspaper edited by one Felicity Cross, ninth-grader.

I wouldn't have known about the article if Alex hadn't shown me a copy during lunch. Sure, hearing all those, "We don't blame you, Sarah!" shouts during the morning seemed a little strange but *everything* seemed that way lately so the remarks didn't truly register.

I had hid in the house the rest of that Sunday. I didn't climb out of my uniform until I smelled worse than Piggy Barnes ever could. The stench was gotten rid of by a long, hot bubble bath. Then I trooped downstairs for cocoa and fudge cookies.

Mom was awake and dad's client had canceled. I mumbled that the game had been a rout. Guess they figured losing was the reason for my bad mood because they didn't ask a single question (I never once thought they might be quiet for some other reason). Losing was only half the reason for my depression. I was mad because I never got into the stupid game! Maybe my goaltending could have stopped the Tornadoes. It couldn't have been worse than Steve's, yet Mr. Darrow kept him in for the entire game.

I thought things would be brighter in the morning but they weren't. Gayle didn't show at the corner so I had to trudge to school alone. And I nearly slid down Waverly, which was a sheet of bumpy ice.

At school, I received the terrific news that I'd flunked another science test. Seeing the 53 percent scrawled in blood red didn't exactly make me whoop for joy. The paper would have to be signed by my parents. They aren't fanatics about me getting straight A's but they aren't pleased when I fail. The teacher suggested, "Sarah, you'd better buckle down or we will start blaming you!" When he said it, I still didn't know about the dumb article.

I was sitting alone in the cafeteria, munching absently on a hot dog and wondering if Gayle was sick, when Alex dashed over. He waved sheets of mimeographed paper at me.

"Hi, famous person! Okay if I sit with a celebrity?"

"It's a free country."

"Tch. Tch. A famous person sounding so sarcastic! Won't do for your image."

"What do you want?" I screeched. Fortunately, everyone screeches in the lunchroom so no one paid extra attention.

"You haven't seen *Cross Words* yet?"

"*Cross Words?*" I repeated. "Is that a new quiz show?" Then I remembered. David Underwood wrote for that student newspaper.

Alex tossed the mimeographed sheets on the table. "Sarah, you're front page news. Go ahead, read it!"

I did. Four times before it sunk in.

"That ought to wake up the team, huh?"

"This—this doesn't make any sense!"

"Sure it does! Sarah, you were the only one who wasn't responsible for that lousy game. Maybe Felicity will give you the *Words of Cross Medallion!* That's an honor, you know. She gives it to the subject of the best story of the month."

"Thrills," I muttered, pushing the hot dog away. It was one honor I could do without.

All afternoon, the headline haunted me. *Don't Blame Sarah Dunes!* Why would Felicity Cross, someone I've never spoken to in my life, do that kind of thing to me?

"No! No! Your stitches are all wrong! You'll have to rip them out!" Miss Mitchum yelled.

I glanced up at her and there was a satisfied smirk on her face. She'd been looking for a chance to scold me ever since that day I left to go to practice. As much as I yearned to scream back, "Want to see some real ripping, *Miz* Mitchum!" and then proceed to yank off her purple beehive, I didn't. I simply ripped out the wrong stitches and was about to start basting again when the door opened. Coach Caplan.

"Practice!" I dumped my material into my large brown envelope and hurried over to her. Practice hadn't been originally scheduled for this afternoon but after the way we played yesterday, Mr. Darrow made certain he could rent out a rink.

I expected another scene from Miss Mitchum but all she did was clear her throat a few times and glower at us. I followed the coach. When we reached the staircase, she put her hand on my arm.

"Sarah, Mr. Darrow told me to get you but I'm questioning his wisdom at the moment." She pursed her lips then said quietly, "There isn't any real need for you to attend the practice today. I'll take full responsibility for excusing you."

"I don't get it. Since I didn't play yesterday, I really need the work."

"That's just it."

"What do you mean?" My throat was starting to feel like a sour ball was stuck in it.

She stared at the birdcage rungs which separated the "Up" stairs from the "Down" ones. "Sarah, I'm afraid the *Cross Words* article was read by everyone on the team. And just now, *to* everyone."

"To—to everyone?"

"Mr. Darrow thought that after the horrid performance we put on against the Tornadoes, the team needed to be shaken up. Everyone else was already in the parking lot and he decided to read the article aloud."

I'm not totally dense. I knew the team reaction without her spelling it out. It's like when you've done something wrong and your folks recite some corny parable to you, in which some kid made exactly the right move to the wrong one you had made. That always irritated me and made me want to strangle the kid in the parable. In this case, I'm the one people would want to strangle.

"I guess I won't play against the Mavericks next week. So, I suppose practice today is unnecessary."

"I'm glad you understand, Sarah. Go back to your class."

And she left. Instead of going back to sewing, I headed for the fourth floor library. Anyone can go in and out of there without a pass. I knew David Underwood worked in

66

the library this period. He was wheeling a cart around when I arrived.

"David, I need some help."

He didn't ask what I was doing there or anything else. He just said, "Sure, what is it?"

"Where's the headquarters of *Cross Words?*"

He nodded. "So, you saw the article. I'm sorry, Sarah. I didn't know she was going to write something like that. Felicity's secretive about her headline material." David sighed. "Felicity is kind of weird, Sarah."

"Then we ought to get along swell. Where is she?" Ninth graders have free periods during seventh. I knew she had to be working on her newspaper. The kids said she was always working on her newspaper.

"Third floor, near the science labs. There's a small room, used to be a supply closet. You can't miss it."

"Thanks, David."

The door was closed but he was right, I couldn't miss it. In day-glo colors was a sloppily scrawled sign tacked haphazardly to the door, *Cross Words Spoken Here.* I wondered what Felicity would've done if her name had been Johnson? I didn't bother to knock.

The room was a worse mess than my room. There were papers strewn all over the place, magic markers formed an obstacle course on the floor, and McDonald's bags decorated two rusty file cabinets.

At first, I didn't think there was any human life within. I was half-right—Felicity Cross sat at a desk. She's short, fat, with splotches of acne and she wears braces across the biggest buck teeth I've ever seen. She reeked of *eau de Piggy*. And I knew instantly we wouldn't get along. I'm weird. Felicity Cross is gross.

"If you're looking to work on my esteemed publication, you're out of luck. You don't look like a writer, anyway. Are you a garbage monitor?" She stuffed french fries in her mouth.

"You mean, you don't recognize me, Felicity?" I said, striding over to her desk and towering over it and her. Sometimes, it pays to be tall. This was a sometimes.

"Should I? Mmmm, I get it! You're running for office!"

"Yeah. I ran all the way to *this* office."

But she was too stoned on french fries and Big Macs so my words went over her head.

"You're being extremely vague," she said testily. "Not that I'm not good at guessing games. I'm wonderful at everything I do," she said, taking a gulp from a thick shake. It left a chocolate moustache on her. She didn't wipe it away. "Look, I have eight haikus and two editorials to write. I simply cannot be bothered by trivial matters."

"Felicity! I'm surprised at you! I'm Sarah Dunes! You know, of *Don't Blame* fame."

She grinned wildly, showing potatoes enmeshed in her braces. "Great! You don't have to thank me for the article.

It was brilliant, I know. You came here for an exclusive interview, didn't you?" She frowned. "I suppose my readers will understand four haikus instead of eight." She whipped out a Coke-stained pad and picked up a magic marker off the floor. "Okay, shoot."

"Don't tempt me."

"What? You're going to have to be much less vague in an interview, Sarah."

I leaned over and was nose to nose with her. "I intend to be, Felicity. Here's the exclusive—goalies rarely score goals. But I promise you, Felicity Cross, the next game I play, I'm going to score a goal. *I swear.*"

"Fabulous!"

"There's one small catch. I'm going to use your tubby little body as the puck!" And I tossed the remaining french fries on her greasy hair.

You're crazy, I told myself on the way home. You've never spoken like that to anyone, not even a miserable creature like Felicity. *What if she tells someone?* And you've never cut a class before. *What if Miss Mitchum finds out you didn't attend the workout?*

"No practice today?" Dad said when I walked in.

"Practice makes perfect. Who wants to be perfect?"

8

I listened to the radio, expecting to hear, "There's an APB on Sarah Dunes. She is wanted in connection with skipping her sewing class. Her excuse was a hockey practice. However, she also skipped that. Ms. Dunes is 13½, five-feet-seven-inches tall, has short black hair and gray eyes. Anyone knowing the whereabouts of Ms. Dunes is to call this station. We advise extreme caution should you come in contact with this person. We have reason to believe she may become dangerous and use any available human as a live hockey puck."

But the guy on the radio didn't say that; he said we'd have temperatures in the low twenties. I shut off the radio and left my room. Sir L was on top of the staircase, cleaning himself.

"Think you could teach Piggy and Felicity that trick?"

He blinked his sleepy eyes, meowed loudly and went back to preening himself.

"I figured you'd say that."

Dad had a sketch pad on the kitchen counter. Surrounding his sneakered feet were a dozen rumpled sheets of paper. "Your mother's going to be late again."

"Again?" I sighed and shrugged. "Hey, did you tell her about working for Veronique Boutique?"

"Mmmm." He kept drawing. Artists aren't supposed to be disturbed but this artist also happens to be a dad so he tends to get interrupted a lot while working.

"Bet she threw a fit, huh?"

"You're certainly in a better mood now than when you arrived home."

"Yeah, well, I'm not wanted dead or alive."

"*What?*" He dropped his pencil.

I picked it up and handed it to him. "Not important. Tell me about mom's reaction."

"If you say so, Sarah." He sighed and closed the sketch pad. "My work isn't going as planned, anyway. Your mother wasn't exactly elated over my job with Veronique but your mother and I have an open relationship, Sarah."

"Which translates—mom said, hands on hips, 'Winston, you're free to do what you want. And if you choose to work for *those* people, then, by all means, do so!' " And I tried to sound deep and sultry the way she does. Only I went too deep and choked.

Dad laughed. "That was about the way it was."

"Did you design those Christmas cards yet?"

"Sure did. It was a rush job. I'm working on summer brochures now."

I pored over the sketches, even the ones on the kitchen floor. "I like your cartoons better."

"These are more profitable at the moment." He tweaked my nose. Even though he knows he's a terrific cartoonist, he likes to be complimented now and again.

"Anything else new?" I asked, going to the fridge. I grabbed a container of strawberry yogurt.

"Got a letter from your Aunt Rosiland. She'll be here a few days before Christmas."

"Right. It's an every-other-Christmas."

"What say we go out to dinner?"

Usually, I'd jump at the chance. Dad loves junk food as much as I do but most of the kids hang around McDonald's, the pizza parlor, and the Dairy Queen. I didn't feel up to another chorus of *"Don't Blame Sarah Dunes!"*

"Nah, I have a lot of homework."

Dad looked at me funny; he knows homework, a little or a lot, never stops me from going out to eat. He didn't press me about it. Instead, he offered to pick up some goodies and bring them home. I went for that suggestion.

"Don't forget the Rocky Road from Baskin-Robbins!" I shouted as he strode up the street.

"Ouch!" Dad yelled.

"What's wrong?" I stepped onto the lawn and shivered. Felt like twenty degrees *below!*

"I tripped! The street has bumps all over it!"

"That's probably why they named it Waverly."

"Sarah, go do your 'lot of homework.' "

I grinned, locked the door, grabbed my yogurt and watched "Star Trek."

When I went to school the next day, I'd almost forgotten about yesterday's terrible happenings. *Almost.*

"Where's your signed test paper?" my science teacher demanded.

"Signed test paper?"

"You know, the 53 percent?"

"Oh, *that* test paper. Um, I forgot."

Then in English, I found out we had to read another book. I wouldn't have minded so much if Mrs. Jacobs hadn't passed out a list of titles and I realized that none had been made into movies. Visions of six hundred pages covered in maroon *and* hunter green danced in my head.

I stopped by Gayle's house on the way home. Mrs. Steinberg answered the door. She's a small woman, with a mass of coppery curls, all done just right by her hairdresser. She's a nice lady, too, except when she's teaching piano. That's why I was surprised at her appearance at the door. Her hair was straight and thatches of gray showed at her roots. She scowled at me.

"Sarah, Gayle is not up to visitors." And she actually started to shut the door!

In my most polite voice, I said, "I'm sorry to hear that, Mrs. Steinberg. She seemed fine at the dance Saturday night."

"Saturday night. Saturday night." Mrs. Steinberg shook her head. "Yes, Sarah, she was fine earlier in the evening but she took ill later. I'm sure she'll explain everything when she returns to school. Now if you will excuse me . . ." And she slammed the door.

Why did I get the feeling Gayle wasn't sick-sick but upset about something? Probably the same thing that had upset her a few weeks back. How I wished she'd talk to me! She always said I was a good listener. Maybe not good enough for whatever was getting her down now. I gave a last glance at the Steinberg house and trudged home. At least I could talk to Connie tonight!

But Connie quickly dashed those hopes. "Tony's home. If I talk on the phone long, he'll snitch and tell mama and pop that I was talking instead of studying."

Her test for St. Catherine's was Saturday morning. We made a date to meet at Wo Luck's at one, after my appointment with Dr. Marangi. I could tell her everything then. No sooner had I hung up than the phone rang. My spirits soared. It had to be Gayle.

It wasn't. The voice on the other end belonged to my Aunt Rhonda. "Mom's not home yet, Rhonda," I said.

"You're the one I want to talk to, Sarah."

"Oh."

"First, tell me about the Tornado game."

"I didn't play," I said hurriedly. Thought that would stop the flow of questions but I should've known better!

"Discrimination! You should fight it. Do you want me to help?"

"I'm glad I didn't play," I lied. "We got clobbered."

"If you'd been in the net, you would've shut them out! Clear case of discrimination. Can't you see . . ."

I allowed her to "prattle on" (mom's description of her monologues).

"All right! I said my piece," she said when she finished her three minute (I timed it) speech. "I shall now explain the *real* reason for this call." She sucked in her breath then giggled. "Sarah, I've met the most divine guy!"

Suddenly, I was interested. Rhonda goes through boyfriends the way I go through thick shakes. "You have?"

"Yes! He's wonderful, super, fantastic, etc. And he's a big, *big* hockey fan. He even went to Lake Placid and saw the gold medal win."

"Wow!" I was impressed.

"That's not all, Sarah. In fact, he has tickets for the Ranger game the Sunday night after this coming one."

The Rangers were on the road this weekend. Who were they playing next? I knew their schedule as well as I knew the Dolphins'. It hit me. *"The Canadiens!"*

"The Canadiens are coming! The Canadiens are coming!" Dad called from downstairs. I'd gotten too loud.

"Super! Oh, you're so lucky, Rhonda."

"We're both lucky, Sarah. He has *three* tickets. I told him all about you."

"*Wow!*" I screamed.

When I came downstairs dad remarked that Wow better be worth having his eardrums punctured. Quickly, I told him about Rhonda's invitation. He said it was fine by him but to check it with mom. "If she ever decides to come home early enough for you to talk to her. At least she's got a day off this week. Want to pick up the turkey with me?"

Mom has a day off this week. A turkey. That could only mean one thing. Thanksgiving. The signed test paper wasn't the only thing I'd forgotten about. Thanksgiving had totally slipped my mind. Usually, dismissing such a big holiday (not to mention two whole days off from school) would be unusual but with the way my mind was working lately, I wasn't surprised I'd forgotten about it.

Thanksgiving is never a big deal at our house. Except for the meal. Mom does a great job on the turkey and even bakes an apple pie from scratch. Dad and I spend the day cracking walnuts and watching football. We don't usually have company; mom invited Rhonda (and told her the Ranger game was okay) and her new boyfriend but they had plans. So, it was just the three of us, which was kind of nice.

Since Connie was busy studying and Gayle remained incognito, I found myself with nothing to do. That's probably why I jumped at the chance to go to the movies and hamburgers afterwards with Susie, a girl in my science class, who had, up to the time she phoned me, never spoken more than two words to me in class. She's very popular and belongs to the cheerleading squad and debating society. Obviously, a very *normal* type person and she must think me that way, too.

She didn't. I found out she had an ulterior motive for becoming "friends" with me. Sarah Dunes was not only big news at school, thanks to Felicity's stupid story, but Sarah Dunes also knew "gorgeous, hunky" Steve Hollaway. She wanted a formal introduction, which I thought was stupid since Steve's not formal at all. Now, it would've been easy enough for me to say, "Sure, come to the Maverick game Sunday and I'll introduce you." But something stopped me.

"Steve and I are avowed enemies," I said after remembering I hadn't seen her at the Topsy-Turvy Dance. "We never, *ever* speak."

Susie said she'd forgotten about cheerleading practice and could we stop for hamburgers some other time? I got the message. Maybe I should've been insulted but I wasn't. And I was happy that I wouldn't be the one to introduce her to Steve.

The time alone gave me a chance to clear my muddled brain. I came up with a surefire way to get out of the team doghouse.

On the ride over to the Maverick rink, I sat next to Russ

in the back seat. I usually sit with Coach Caplan but Piggy had elected to be up front. Even though it was twenty-two degrees, the Coach had the window by the driver's seat wide open.

"Hi, Russ. Cold out, huh?" I open conversations brilliantly.

"Hi, yourself, 'Blameless.' "

That again! But as I said, I had a way out of it. "Guess where I'm going next Sunday night?"

"Where?" Russ asked.

"To the Garden."

"The Garden?" He raised a bushy eyebrow. Then he whistled. "Fan-tastic! Rangers are playing Montreal."

"Yeah, and if the Rangers win and the Islanders lose to Philly, the Rangers get sole possession of first place."

"Hey, did you hear that?" Russ shouted to the others. "Sarah's going to the Garden next week."

And that did it. Got me out of the doghouse. Everyone asked for programs, yearbooks, and I promised to deliver if they gave me the money, of course.

We also managed to tie the mighty Mavericks, 3–3. I didn't get to play but the *"Don't Blame Sarah Dunes"* monkey was off my back.

On the way home, the kids were singing and whooping. I just sat by the window and smiled into the dusk. My life might return to normal.

9

My optimism was short-lived.

Wrestling an English book out of my locker, I heard Alex's voice. Only when I turned around, he wasn't there. Well, he was and he wasn't. My eyes faced dirty tiled walls but my nose came in line with fuzzy blond hair.

Since when was I taller than Alex? "Please tell me you're standing in a hole or that there's a mountain growing in this building and I'm standing atop it."

"It's you, Sarah. You keep getting taller and taller!" And he threw his head back in exaggerated fashion to look up at me.

"Ha. Ha. Very funny!" Was my height the reason Alex had lost interest in me this year?

"I just came from English and you know that book report our classes have to do?" Alex has Mrs. Jacobs first period.

"It's not due today? Alex, don't tell me that." I slumped against my locker.

"No! Just thought you'd like to know we don't have to

hand in a regular report. At least my class doesn't. And Mrs. Jacobs usually has all her eighth grade—"

"Whoa! We don't have to hand in a 'regular report.' Does that mean we have to give it orally?" Speaking in front of a class doesn't bother me—like in September when I went from homeroom to homeroom announcing tryouts for the Blue Dolphins. But giving a book report orally—that makes me want to develop terminal chicken pox.

"Not that, either."

"Alex! I don't have time for 'Twenty Questions.' "

"Okay. The report still has to be written but it has to be done in the style of a movie review. You know, 'Four Stars. One of the Year's Ten Best,' like they have in the newspaper ads. Mrs. Jacobs will fill you in."

"That's crazy. None of the books on the list are movies!" I sighed. "Thanks for the warning, Alex. I'll see you in sewing."

I seriously wondered if Mrs. Jacobs had gotten the idea for the movie review from my last book report. No! I was becoming paranoid, as Gayle would say. As I wondering on the cafeteria line, I saw David. He said he'd called Gayle several times but Mrs. Steinberg always answered and wouldn't bring Gayle to the phone. The whole situation was becoming curiouser and curiouser, like in *Alice in Wonderland*.

On Friday afternoon, Coach Caplan said, "Don't forget that full report on the Ranger game."

"Or the programs and pennants and yearbooks," I said, patting my tote bag bulging with change and bills. "Um, could you do me a favor?" Something had been bothering me since my meeting with Alex.

"If I can."

When I told her, she smiled and went into her tiny office. I stood against the wall.

"Stop slouching! I can't measure you properly if you slouch!" She measured me. "Five-feet-seven-and-one-quarter inches."

"How high are the ceilings?" I asked, reaching up and touching them.

Coach laughed. "Sarah, your height is a great asset! If I wasn't so short, I would've pursued a *real* career in hockey. Your size is the main reason I think you have an excellent future in the sport. Tall goaltenders are in demand. And the taller you are, as a girl, your chances can only be enhanced."

I wrinkled my nose. *My future in hockey . . . As a girl.* She sounded an awful lot like Rhonda. But something else she said had struck a nerve. My height was the *main* reason for my future in hockey.

"You mean, I better keep growing or I won't be any good? I thought the only reason I'm backup to Steve is because he's better. Not because he's taller and I'm shorter!"

"Sarah! Calm down! You're getting all red in the face and you're not making sense. You know what I meant."

"Well, maybe I'll grow taller than everyone else in the school! Taller than the high school kids! Wouldn't that be terrific!"

And I walked out. Coach Caplan wasn't the person I thought her to be. She wasn't on my side!

I brooded all evening. Mom shocked us by coming home early. I was all set to go downstairs to meet her but her voice carried all the way up to my room. "You mean she's squirreled away in her room *again?*"

Dad mumbled something I couldn't make out and mom replied, "Adolescence should be synonymous with weirdness."

See, even my own mother thinks of me as Sarah Dunes, Weird Person.

"Very good checkup, Sarah," Dr. Marangi said Saturday after cleaning my teeth. "Just be careful you don't lose any of these in the hockey rink. I don't want to see you again for six months."

"I've never gotten hurt playing hockey!" I didn't count Piggy's assault.

He chuckled and yanked off the bib. "Maybe not yet

but I've seen too many injuries in school sports. Did you know that I got into college via a football scholarship?"

"You're kidding!" Dr. Marangi looks more like Woody Allen than Earl Campbell.

"When I was in college, Sarah, it wasn't necessary to weigh over two hundred pounds or be over six feet to participate in sports. Anyhow," a big grin crossed his thin face, "I was the field-goal kicker."

I laughed and he told me not to eat too much junk food and to have a nice Christmas.

When I left his office, I felt better than I'd felt in a couple of days. Connie would be at Wo Luck's in awhile. I had time to stroll around the village and look at the Christmas decorations.

The village reminds me of one of those Austrian or Bavarian towns they're always showing on "Wide World of Sports." "Quiet and nestled in . . ." That just about described the village. I went past the optician, the pizza parlor and stood for one glorious minute outside the side-by-side bakeries. One was Italian and one Jewish and the aromas made me dizzy. I was really hungry! But it wasn't even one yet so I continued my slow walk.

I found myself in front of fancy gold lettering that announced to the world that this store was different from the rest in the village. Veronique Boutique.

When I entered the cluttered and heavily perfumed shop, a tall, outrageously skinny woman, with huge yellow eyeglasses (frame and lenses), pounced on me. "Yes?" she said in a high-pitched nasal twang.

"I'm just looking."

"For what?" she snapped.

I guess my workboots, jeans, and sleeve-torn ski jacket didn't go with the Oscar de la Renta gown I was standing next to.

"Don't touch a thing!"

I walked out. Seem to be doing that a lot lately. How could dad work for such a snob outfit? He'd do better by drawing cartoons of Eyeglasses. I'd suggest it to him when I got home.

I backtracked to the middle of the village. There stood a scrawny and unhappy looking Christmas tree. Or was it me who was scrawny and unhappy? I turned the corner by Wo Luck's. Mr. Steinberg was coming out of the restaurant.

"Sarah, how you doing?" he said cheerfully.

"Terrific," I lied. The incident at Veronique had really dampened my spirits. "Is Gayle feeling better?"

He scratched his beard. "Feeling better? Um . . ."

"Yeah, well, being out of school for two weeks . . . um, I guess you're really sick then," I mumbled the last part because Mr. Steinberg continued to scratch his beard and his eyes had narrowed.

"Out for two weeks. Sarah, she'll be back on Monday. Nice seeing you."

As I watched him hurry away, I realized he hadn't

known Gayle had been out of school. But Mrs. Steinberg knew. . . .

I entered the restaurant and asked the waiter for a booth for two.

Mrs. Steinberg knew and Mr. Steinberg didn't?

"I think I'm in!"

The other diners looked up and laughed. Under all her blonde hair, Connie's face was flushed and she seemed to be moving in ten directions at once.

"Big deal," I muttered, nibbling on the noddles the waiter had provided the moment I sat down.

"Big deal? Fantastic deal! Oooh, am I hungry! Sarah, I was a wreck but once I read the first question, I knew I'd be okay."

"Order now?" The waiter reappeared. *He knows us. If he doesn't take the order straight off, we go through two bowls of noodles deciding.* Since he stood there, pencil poised over pad, we had no choice but to tell him what we wanted. I ordered shrimp fried rice, Connie picked pepper steak, and we both had egg drop soup. During the latter, Connie told me all about the test. It sounded impossible to me but then I didn't know any of the religious answers. Or the science. Or the math. . . .

"So, what's new with you?" she asked breathlessly.

"Enough," I said, hiding the noodles behind the bottle of soy sauce. *The waiter tries to take off with the noodles but I always outfox him. One time, I put them under the table but then forgot they were there and stuck my sneak-*

ers in them. That's when I figured out the behind-the-soy-sauce-bottle trick. Actually, if the truth be known, Gayle figured it out. *Gayle.* Should I tell Connie about my meeting with Mr. Steinberg? No, no sense in stepping on her good mood.

I skipped over the rotten parts of my life; therefore, I managed to tell her all my news before eating half my rice.

"What about Christmas?" she asked, mushing a green pepper in sauce.

"What about it?"

"Shopping, Sarah! Want to go with me? I've saved up my allowance since September. How about you?" She popped the mushed pepper in her mouth.

"Sure, to your first question. And to your second, you know I don't get a regular allowance. I need to buy an extra present this year. My Aunt Rosiland's coming to visit."

"What are you getting from your parents?"

I paused in the middle of stabbing a shrimp. "I don't have any idea." True, mom had brought home all those packages the day she gave me the skirt and sweater set but those were "usual" presents—pajamas, a robe, flannel shirts, and boring stuff like that. I got those every year. My folks usually hounded me for two months before Christmas for the really special gift I wanted. They hadn't hounded this year. What was weirder, though, was I didn't have any special present in mind.

"I'm getting a new tape recorder!" Connie said excitedly. "One with a digital counter and pause button. Mama and pop promised me one if I passed the test—"

"You don't know for sure if you did," I cautioned.

"I'll know for sure before Christmas. They're going to give me the recorder so I can practice for next year when I'm working on St. Catherine's radio station."

Talk about confidence! Connie's not even definitely in St. Catherine's and she knows she'll be on the radio staff. I'm on the Dolphins this year and after Coach Caplan's comments yesterday, I'm not sure if I'll even be a member of the team next year!

"I hope Gayle invites us to a Hanukkah service again."

I sipped my strong tea. Last winter had been *so* different. We'd just moved here and within days, I was over at Gayle's house, joining in on her holiday festivities, meeting Connie, and Alex took me to a Christmas party. Sir Lancelot had adopted us. And the most important at the time, I learned that in the eighth grade, I could try out for the hockey squad. How nice everything had been . . .

"Sarah!" Connie whispered urgently. "You're dribbling on the tablecloth!"

"Ooops!" Wiping myself off, I said, "I hope this Christmas turns out like the last."

But I wasn't taking bets on it.

10

On Sunday, I rode the train into New York City. The car was an old one, with straw popping out of the seat. Heat chugged from underneath the seat, forcing me to keep my legs on the seat instead of dangling over. The wheels made a click-click-sputter sound and we didn't exactly whiz by the countryside; we chugged.

You're embarking on a strange and mysterious journey, Sarah Dunes, I told myself. This train isn't really going to New York City. You're being kidnapped to an outer planet where no one thinks you're weird and you're the best goaltender since Ken Dryden.

I almost convinced myself of my fantasy until the train plunged into the tunnel in Harlem. No more click-click-sputter but a continuous drone. The lights shone brighter, causing me to squint. So much for pleasant daydreams.

On the upper level of Grand Central Station, I parked myself by a closed Off-Track Betting window. No telling when Rhonda and her dream guy would arrive. Knowing my aunt, it might be two hours late.

"There she is! Isn't she adorable?"

Rhonda fifteen minutes early? She was! "Hi," I said.

As usual, she looked super, all decked out in a sheep-skin jacket and fuzzy pink hat. He looked super, too. He was about Rhonda's height, dark hair, black-rimmed glasses, and a fabulous droopy moustache. I say "he" because I never figured out if his name was Jules, Julie, Jude, or Darling; Rhonda called him the latter all the time.

Whoever he was, I liked him right off. He said hello and told me I looked like Rhonda. ("Didn't I tell you that, Darling? And she's a *marvelous* athlete, too!") Then he said, "I'm starved."

The restaurant was great. Not fancy but kind of homey. Darling explained that the food was a mixture of Middle Eastern cuisines with the majority of the dishes being Greek. But he didn't explain *too* much. Grown-ups often do that. Especially Rhonda's boyfriends. Mom says, "Rhonda brings out the paternal instinct in the male."

Anyhow, I had this saffron rice, which was bright gold and fantastic, moussaka, which was too rich but yummy all the same, and this great tasting flat bread. Throughout the meal, Rhonda "prattled on," but Darling managed to get a word in and include me in the conversation too. I was liking him more and more.

When I finished the honey-soaked dessert, I didn't want to budge but we had to walk to the Garden. I felt like an overstuffed scarecrow as we made our way down Ninth Avenue.

It was dark and icy cold. Sunday evenings in Manhattan resemble the world after Doomsday. Very few people and tall, ugly buildings towering over those people. Darling and Rhonda walked arm-in-arm and I strolled along the curbside until Darling grabbed my arm. Then we all moved together.

Suddenly, Rhonda announced, "Sarah's going to play for the Rangers someday."

"I don't know about that," I mumbled.

"Of course you will! There won't be any discriminatory barriers when you're old enough and if there are, you'll simply bash your way through—"

"Maybe Sarah won't play for the Rangers."

"But Darling, she's a *wonderful* goaltender!" insisted Rhonda who'd never seen me play.

He laughed. "I'm sure Sarah's as wonderful as you say but she may not play for the Rangers for a reason other than discrimination."

"What's that?" Rhonda and I asked in unison.

"Simple. Sarah might get drafted by another team."

I liked his style! It also got us into a discussion of drafting American-born hockey players and the USA gold medal. He was a big Jim Craig fan, too. This time, Rhonda did most of the listening.

If there's anything that makes me nervous, it's an escalator. The disappearing steps remind me of suction tubes. Someday, there'll be a horror film about people being swallowed by angry escalators and the director of the movie will use the fast-moving stairs at Madison Square Garden as an example.

They Zoom and Zap! You place one foot down and before you put the other one down, you're at the next landing! I was glad Darling guided me along.

Our seats were terrific, just a little off center ice so we had a good view of the action. Before the game began, I collected the goodies for the Dolphins. Darling treated me to my own scorecard, program, and yearbook.

If the location was terrific, the game was better. The Canadiens jumped to a one goal lead in the first minute of play and the Garden Boo-Birds got on the Rangers. That irritated me so I cheered louder. Four minutes later, the Rangers scored and the place went wild. Rhonda was on her feet, screaming and pounding Darling on the back. I just put my fingers in my mouth and whistled.

Both goaltenders were having great games. The Montreal goalie made seventeen saves in the scoreless second period while the Rangers' netminder made fifteen.

The third period whizzed by. The Rangers hit the post twice and everyone groaned and moaned. There was less than a minute to play, the score still deadlocked one-all. The crowd stood as one.

Twenty seconds to go. The Rangers rushed up ice. A

Canadien winger poke-checked the puck but before he could get to the Rangers' blue line, the Rangers recaptured.

Ten seconds on the clock. The Rangers were over the Montreal blue line. The puck was shot. The goalie made the initial save. But the rebound wasn't cleared.

Two seconds . . .

The Rangers' center flicked the puck into the upper left hand corner.

The Garden went bananas. The Boo-Birds turned into Turtledoves and everyone was hugging everyone else. Pandemonium on the ice, too, with all the Rangers congratulating each other.

But my eyes drifted to the other end of the rink, back to where the Canadien goalie stood. He was leaning tiredly on his goal stick, his uniform drenched in sweat and beads of moisture dripped from his mask. The other Canadiens skated past him, en route to the dressing room. But he didn't budge. He was totally alone.

I knew how he felt.

11

Mom and dad were deathly silent during breakfast the next morning. I decided to liven things up. "I had a great time at the game. What do you think of Rhonda's Darling?" He'd driven me back and they'd visited with my parents. He and Rhonda were still here long after I went to bed.

"Mmmm . . ." was all mom said.

"Dammit! My toast is burning!" from dad.

I joined the ranks of the deathly silent.

Wind zipped through Waverly. I had to walk hunched over, like a swaying, skinny tree. The noise of the wind blotted out all other sounds, including the sounds of my own footsteps, so when something/someone thumped me on the shoulder, I nearly went into orbit.

"Hi, it's only me. Didn't mean to scare you."

"*Gayle!*"

"Bingo," she said but she didn't smile.

I remember seeing her dad in the village and wanted to question her about him not knowing she was home from school for two weeks but from the way she drop-kicked a pebble over a fence, I figured it was a good idea to keep my mouth shut. Gayle's temper can match her mother's and I didn't want to be booted over a fence.

At practice, I handed out the souvenirs of the Ranger game. The whole team had listened to the game but they demanded a firsthand account of the action. I'm not as good as Connie is at doing play-by-play but I did my best. They seemed satisfied. The "Don't Blame Sarah Dunes" monkey was officially off my back.

Dad met me outside the rink. I hadn't expected him. Mom was working late *again*, he said. We went out for dinner. We stopped off at the DQ and brought home banana splits for dessert (no matter how cold it gets, I can always eat ice cream). Mom was home when we arrived.

"Junk food! Look at the McDonald's napkins stuffed in your pockets! From Sarah, I expect it, but not from you, Winston!"

"Hi, Mom," I said.

"Well, you're never home for dinner and going out is more fun than hanging around waiting for you to put in an appearance."

"My job keeps me busy. And I am home *now*."

"Terrific, you're home at 8:15 instead of 9:15. I guess I should be thankful for small favors," Dad said, dropping the DQ bag on the kitchen counter.

"It's starting to snow. Dad thinks we'll have a real storm. I tried to catch snowflakes in my mouth—"

"I have a TV dinner in the oven. There's a Cary Grant movie on at nine."

"That's why you're home early!"

"World War III erupted in Moscow today," I said.

Mom strode over to the TV set and put it on full blast. Dad picked out his banana split and half of it ended up on the floor. Without waiting for my dessert, I snuck away to my room.

I clutched my pillow to my chest. Couldn't mom come home a little earlier? She was the boss, after all. But maybe being the boss forced her to work so much over-time. Then couldn't dad be a little more sympathetic even though he missed her so much? Sir L purred in my ear and the soothing sound lulled me to sleep.

Gayle was more communicative as the week wore on but she still wasn't her usual self. She spoke what people call polite conversation. "Isn't the snow nice?" (Not if you live on Waverly. I tripped all the way to the corner.) "The science test was easier than I thought." (I managed a 67 percent by picking the right answer in a multiple choice.) Stuff like that. Like we were strangers—which at this point, I felt we were. I was glad when Connie invited me over for dinner Thursday night. It was a welcome break in my suddenly monotonous schedule. No more parties, going to movies or roller skating (there's an indoor rink nearby). I really missed the super things I used to take for granted. Of course, hockey season had a lot to do with it.

I guess Connie, Gayle, and I were all wrapped up in different things. Only I wished I knew what Gayle was involved in.

Test Tube Tony was out somewhere, much to my delight. Jimmy and I played two games of checkers and he won both. Then Mrs. Russo insisted it was his bedtime. His wails reached Connie and me in the kitchen, where we were loading up the dishwasher.

"Have you spoken to Gayle?" Connie asked.

"I think so."

"You think so?"

"Well, I spoke to someone. It looked like Gayle, it walked like Gayle, but I'm not totally convinced it was Gayle."

"Think I know what you mean. I phoned her and invited her along on our Christmas shopping spree—she does buy Hanukkah presents, you know—but she said no and changed the subject. Real abrupt-like. Then she mumbled a few silly things about the weather, a new record, and then she said her mother wanted to speak to her. You know her mother never bothers her while she's on the phone. Do you think she's in trouble, Sarah?"

"Trouble?"

"I don't mean 'in trouble' like they say in those old movies. I mean in some kind of a mess. Maybe her parents don't approve of that Ralph you told me about. Or maybe she's smoking grass again."

The *again* threw me. I didn't know Gayle had ever smoked. At least not as long as I'd known her. Connie had been friends with her for several years, though.

"She tried it the summer before you came here," Connie said, reading my mind. "And her parents caught her. She was grounded for a whole month. And you know how she hasn't been going anywhere lately."

I shook my head. "No, her folks wouldn't keep her home from school."

"Well, that's one theory up in smoke."

" 'Up in smoke'! I think I'm going to be ill!" I grabbed my stomach and hobbled around the kitchen.

"*Mamma mia!* My food was good. I made the pasta from scratch! Sarah, are you all—"

At the sound of Mrs. Russo's voice, I straightened up. "Your food was terrific."

"Mama, we were just talking and Sarah thought something I said was gross."

Mrs. Russo smiled. "As long as it wasn't my cooking. My daughter's talking, okay, my food, never."

How did such a sweet woman ever give birth to Test Tube Tony?

The Blue Dolphins had recovered from the Tornado massacre and buoyed by the tie with the Mavericks, we were again looking like a team vying for the number one spot in our division. Steve's reflexes were sharper than ever and Piggy's shots grew accurate again. Against a fierce team like the Yellow Jackets, or the YJs as everyone called them, it was mandatory that we be at the peak of our game.

And we were the afternoon of the confrontation. Even the chilling sleet and the fact that neither Connie nor Gayle nor my parents would be in the stands, could cloud my anticipation of this contest.

The YJ rooters are loud and perhaps the most rabid junior high fans around. I couldn't even hear my pen scratching on the shots-on-goal chart.

Going into the second period, the score was tied, one-one. I calculated the YJs had fifteen shots on Steve, seven of which were really tough stops for him to come up with.

I started to add up our shots when the YJs broke up ice. To a normal observer, the play didn't look *that* dangerous but I knew how Steve saw it. Two forwards zooming, one trailing slightly, while the center was bulling his way past our defense. Any one of the trio could shoot the puck or pass it. I held my breath.

The right-winger was no sooner in our zone than he let go with a quick wrist shot. Steve's leg kicked out, his pads preventing the puck from going in. But there was something else—Steve fell on that outstretched leg.

And he didn't move.

From my perch on the bench, I glanced up at Coach Caplan. She muttered, "Oh, God."

No one had to tell me what to do. The pen and clipboard were turned over to our extra defenseman and I hopped over the boards. Steve was being helped to the bench, his left leg not touching the ice; his face was hidden by his mask but I knew he was grimacing.

"I don't think it's broken," he muttered.

"Yeah," was all I could say. I skated toward the net and the arena broke into whistles and jeers.

"Lookit the girl goalie!"

"Bet she wears a mask to cover her ugly face!"

"Why don't you go home and play with your Barbie doll?"

I should explain that the YJs are an all-boy team and that their junior high does its best to steer girls away from the hockey team.

"Don't blow it, Dunes."

"Thanks for the vote of confidence, Piggy," I said, smoothing out the chipped ice in front of me.

It wasn't until play was ready to resume, in the circle to my left, that I realized I, Sarah Dunes, Weird Person, was in my first game of the season, against the toughest opponent we had.

Suddenly, there wasn't any time for realizing. The YJ center got the puck back to the point and a shot flew. I froze; fortunately, the shot went way wide.

Get with it, Sarah!

The action went the other way but I didn't have a

chance to catch my breath. The YJs recaptured at the blue line and were back in our territory.

They had their high scoring line out against our best checkers, the puck game going back and forth, from blue uniforms to gold. Getting dizzy was only half my problem. The other half was made up of YJ#4, who'd planted himself in front of the cage. My defense had vanished. Actually, ran for safety is a better description. YJ#4 is six feet and two hundred pounds.

Now, maybe I should've known better but he was infringing on my crease. So I did what any other self-respecting goalie would do. I tattooed him with my stick.

He cursed and tried to retaliate. At the same time, a YJ forward took a shot from the sideboards. I kicked out the puck before it crossed the goal line. I also *just happened* to kick old #4. Naturally, he wanted revenge. But he tried for it at the wrong time—after the ref had blown the play dead.

"Yellow Jacket #4, two minutes, high sticking at 15:02."

There was a chorus of boos. Some at me for getting away with a trip but most at the YJ player. After all, taking a penalty in the attacking zone is a no-no.

Russ scored on that power play and we were leading, 2–1 at the end of the second.

Getting into the game had been so totally unexpected that I didn't have a real chance to feel nervous. I was having much too much fun!

The third period was the best, however. I made three tough saves, one on a breakaway and had the good luck of two YJs clanking the post. Piggy and Russ scored a goal each and we beat the feared YJs, 4–1. The YJ supporters were disappointed but they applauded our efforts and what was even more rewarding, there weren't anymore Barbie doll cracks.

"Great game, Sarah!" Russ tapped me on the shoulder.

I ripped off my mask. My face felt like the Mississippi and all its tributaries. "Thanks, I'm just glad we won." Which wasn't altogether truthful. I wasn't just glad about the win. I'd finally gotten into a game!

Coach Caplan hugged me, which must've been a chore since I smelled pretty awful by that time. "I'm so proud of you, Sarah! Especially on that breakaway! You waited 'til the last possible second to make your move!"

"My goals-against-average is *officially* zero now," I said happily. There was another reason to be happy. With Steve injured (though I hoped not seriously) and the Tornado rematch next week, I'd get the starting nod!

The sleet had changed to snow by the time Coach Caplan let me off at the corner. I started up Waverly then stopped. Dad had to go to Veronique Boutique this evening and mom would, of course, be working late again. I had to talk to someone!

What about Gayle? Maybe she'd finally paint on those blue dolphins. Yeah, my mask was okay for a backup goalie but the first-stringer needed a classier act. I dropped off the rest of my equipment at home and mask in hand, went to Gayle's house. I rang the doorbell four times before Gayle answered.

"What are you doing here?"

I walked in, ignoring her less than cordial welcome. "Gayle, I finally got to play! Steve got hurt. Oooh, I was good. *Really* good!"

Gayle slammed the door and I jumped. "Wipe your feet. They're wet."

I did, all the time yakking about the game. It wasn't unusual for her to tell me to wipe my feet. Mrs. Steinberg is touchy about her wall-to-wall carpeting.

". . . so I came here then," I wound up, flopping on the rug (*that* part of me wasn't wet).

"Oh."

Part of me said she wasn't hearing a word I was saying but another part wouldn't allow me to stop talking. The house was too quiet. No Mrs. Steinberg playing the piano, no rock music blaring from the basement. *No anything.*

"Uh, you can put on those dolphins this weekend."

"*What?* What are you *babbling* about?"

Gayle's face was a blank and I wondered if Connie's grass theory had merit. No, this wasn't a stoned blankness. I think there was pain behind the nothingness and that there was something terribly wrong in the Steinberg house. And I didn't want to know what it was.

I spoke quickly, "The dolphins on my mask. You offered to paint them on. I'm sure I'll be in goal next week against the Tornadoes."

"I can't," she said, not revealing any emotion.

"Why not?" I picked at the orange loops of the shag carpet. "I could leave it here . . ."

"No."

". . . over the weekend."

"This weekend I'm going to visit my father."

"Your father? Is he sick, Gayle?" My throat was like the Gobi Desert. "I mean, I saw him last weekend, coming out of Wo Luck's and he looked okay."

She gave a frightening strangled laugh, like a mad-woman in a horror film. I wanted to run home.

"So you're the lousy squealer! I knew it had to be some-body. He showed up here Sunday and spoke to my mother about me returning to school. Thanks a bunch, Sarah Dunes."

Her father *showed up*? She was *going to visit him*?

Then without warning, Gayle loomed over me and screamed, "You and your stupid hockey mask! Can't you ever think of anything or anyone else, Sarah Dunes? I think my parents getting a divorce is a heck of a lot more important than your stupid hockey!"

I would've agreed but she fled from the room.

12

I'd like to say I dashed after Gayle but I didn't. Except for the small area where I sat, the Steinberg house was dark and from past visits, I knew there were five scatter rugs between me and Gayle's room. After what felt like hours but was probably more like two minutes, I stood up, inched my way to where I believed the light switch to be and after some clumsy groping, found it.

The crystal chandelier nearly blinded me but at least I could reach Gayle's room without tripping.

Oh, I suppose I could have ignored the scatter rug obstacle course and hurried after Gayle straight off but to tell the truth, I was temporarily paralyzed. What do you say when your best friend tells you her parents are getting a divorce? Particularly when you don't know any others in the same situation?

That may sound strange since divorces happen all the time. In the city, I had a couple of friends whose parents had split and Alex lives with his mom and stepfather. But none of those kids' folks were in the *process* of splitting up. That's what shook me.

When I reached Gayle's room, I heard her crying in the dark. "Want some water?" I asked brilliantly. If Gayle was anywhere near water, she might drown herself. "Okay if I sit?"

She didn't reply but I crept to where the bed should be. Gayle wasn't on it but on the floor, up near the headboard. There's something comforting about a cold floor when you're upset. I remember from Sir L's illness.

"Do you want to talk about it?"

"Oh, Sarah! They're getting a divorce! *My* parents are getting a divorce!"

I nodded sympathetically, for all the good it did, since Gayle couldn't see the nod.

"Sarah, it's been horrible! All of a sudden, dad started working later and later and then one night, he didn't come home at all and mom was frantic! She was dialing the police when he waltzed in at 3:00 A.M. I was up," she added.

While she was taking a deep breath, I wondered about the way she said, "He waltzed in . . ." She sounded awfully bitter. I wasn't sure I wanted to hear the rest of this. I liked Mr. and Mrs. Steinberg but Gayle seemed to be taking sides. Against her own parents! *Would I?*

"He's got a girlfriend, Sarah! A *girlfriend! My father!*" Gayle crashed something on the floor, possibly a book because it made a noise but didn't shatter. "He told mom he'd been with her. Every night he worked late, he'd been with her. Mom tossed him right out!"

I had a hunch she was about to crash something else, maybe something breakable this time so I jumped in, "Uh, when was all this?"

She sniffled. "I remember exactly. Three days after we came home from our Adirondack trip. The night of your stupid hockey game."

Yeah, that coincided with Gayle's hot and cold behavior. But *why* had she suddenly become happy, her old self again?

Like Connie, Gayle seemed to have the power to read my thoughts. Her voice sounded somewhat calmer. "Then he came back and promised he'd never see *her* again and mom took him back. They said they could work things out. Sarah, it was *soooo* good for awhile. We went everywhere together, more like a real family than we'd been in ages. Know what I mean?"

"Yeah." My own family hadn't been too much of a unit lately.

"Then everything fell apart again! The night of the Topsy-Turvy, a whole gang of kids came back here and we were having a super time. I didn't notice *him* much but he offered to go out for pizza. And was gone a real long time." She gulped. "Then it got to be too late and all the kids went home. *He* didn't return for another two hours.

And do you know where *he* went while we were here waiting? *Do you know where?"*

"Take it easy." She was losing control again.

"No! I've taken it easy too long! Dad—*he* went to see *her*. Imagine that! Of course, mom tossed him out again. Now she has a lawyer handling the whole thing."

"Rough," I muttered. What else could I say? I wanted to help Gayle but there just wasn't a way. "Um, I'm sorry I came over, Gayle."

"I'm glad you know about it, Sarah." She sniffled once more. "I'm sorry I snapped at you about the hockey thing."

"I get carried away sometimes. Listen, you want me to stick around until your mom comes home?"

"No, I'm all right now. As all right as I'll ever be," she mumbled more to herself than to me. In a louder voice, she added, "Sarah, promise me you won't say anything to anyone. Not even Connie."

"Promise. If you need to talk, call."

Gayle didn't say another word; she started sobbing. I stumbled out of the room and ran out of the house.

I was thankful the Blue Dolphins had a 6:30 A.M. ice rental. I couldn't face Gayle this morning; it was too soon.

Everyone was still asleep when I left the house. Snowflakes tattooing my face startled me. Although I hadn't slept much, I hadn't noticed the snow. Several inches covered Waverly. I slipped twice but caught myself before landing on my rear end.

Coach Caplan's Camaro was at the corner. I was the first one she picked up. I collapsed on the front seat and said, "I didn't get much sleep."

"Who can blame you? All the excitement!"

Excitement? How could she know about the Steinbergs? Then I remembered—the Yellow Jacket game. Wow! That almost seemed like it never happened.

"Steve won't be in practice, Sarah."

"He's really hurt?" I asked, smiling. Okay, so it's ghoulish but I couldn't help myself! With Steve out of action, Sarah got into action!

"Enough so he'll miss practice."

I stayed reasonably awake during the workout but once in school . . . I knew I'd nod off sooner or later but why in science?

"Sarah Dunes!"

"Huh? Whaa?" I mumbled. I tried to sit upright and promptly knocked over everything on my desk, which caused the kid in front of me to fall forward and knock over everything on her desk, which caused her to, etc. and in a few seconds, the entire aisle was littered with books, pens, pencils, cigarette packs, and an issue of *Playboy*. I had a feeling my citizenship grade, along with my academic one, had reached an all-time low.

And in English, Mrs. Jacobs reminded us that the movie review-book report was due before Christmas vacation. Two weeks away! I hadn't even picked out a book yet. I'd checked most of the titles at the library and they were all fat, nubby-linen, maroon-covered books. A feeling of doom enveloped me.

It didn't help when I arrived home and there was a note from dad saying he'd be come around five-thirty, he'd bring dinner with him and for me not to budge until he got there. *"Your mother's working late again,"* he wrote, too.

I sat on the counter and poured milk into Sir L's saucer. "Dad's not overly thrilled with mom's late hours."

The cat ignored me and lapped the milk. When he had his fill, he daintily licked his paws.

"I wish I were so single-minded. Food and preening myself. Not another worry in the world."

Worries. Like me and my schoolwork and Gayle with . . .

That wasn't the same thing. I jumped off the counter. Not the same thing at all. My eyes drifted to dad's note. Mom's always working late nowadays. *Just like Gayle's father.*

Stop being such a weird person, Sarah Dunes! Your folks aren't splitting up!

I sacked out on the couch. The aroma of mushrooms and Sicilian pizza woke me up.

"Don't you have a book report? Homework?" Dad said, marching into the kitchen.

"Yeah," I followed him. "Oooh, that smells good!"

"I can reheat it when you're finished with your homework."

I blinked. Dad's not like that. He never gets on me about my schoolwork. Not unless it's really bad, which it was in science but he didn't know . . .

"Your science teacher was irate when he called here this morning."

He knew. "He's always irate," I mumbled.

"No wisecracks, Sarah. You know I don't care if you pull just passing grades. But I don't appreciate getting calls from teachers. I draw the line there. Go upstairs and study. You won't starve," he added when I looked longingly at the pizza.

"Yes, Sir!"

Then dad touched my shoulder. "Sorry, Sarah. I must sound like a tyrant but I've got other things on my mind, too. Do a little studying so you'll get a passing mark in science. And please, try not to fall asleep in class again. He said you snored like a bulldog."

We both laughed and I felt a lot better. Until I got upstairs. *He has other things on his mind?* What things? Mom? Don't get dumb again, Sarah! Mom's always worked late during the holidays.

Not this late and not this often.

I never opened the science book and I never ate the pizza.

13

I spent most of the next afternoon at Connie's. Test Tube Tony made his usual snide remarks, including, "Ain't been asked to any dances lately, eh, Sarah Dune Buggy?" I ignored him. While Connie finished a batch of coconut macaroons, Jimmy and I played two games of Chutes and Ladders. He won both.

"I can't go shopping Saturday," I said, rocking to the beat of an old Rolling Stones record. "I've got a game. But the stores are open Sunday."

"Fine. Gayle will go with us. I called her last night and she said she'd come. Sarah, she sounded different. Not so depressed but not exactly happy, either. In between. Did you notice that?"

Obviously, Gayle hadn't told Connie about the divorce. I'd given my word that I wouldn't but I wondered how long she could keep something like that a secret. "Yeah, I know what you mean about her mood. Those macaroons look delicious."

When I arrived home, there was a surprise, in the form of my mother. I wanted to hug her and yell, "You're not working late! You're not Mr. Steinberg!" But she wouldn't have understood that.

"There's a button off your coat," she said by way of a greeting.

I wasn't wearing my ski jacket. Instead I had on a Greymer & Greymer Junior Jazz navy pea coat. Mom was right. The third button from the top was no longer there. "It's not only off, it's lost to the ages."

"Don't take another age to replace it," she said, peeling a potato. "You used to sew a lot."

"I don't have much time. Hey, but if you can get me some silver bells from the notions department, I'll make time. Wouldn't bells look terrific for Christmas—"

"Sarah! I have a headache. That's the reason I came home early."

Whoopee! I thought it had something to do with the fact she missed us. "Where's dad?"

"At Veronique Boutique. Where else?"

Mom sounded the way a lemon tastes.

Without another word, I set the table. It was clear to me that she had *things* on her mind, too.

Dinner was too quiet. You notice no one talking when there's the clatter of silverware, the constant chewing of hamburgers and the crunching of green beans and french fries. I looked from mom to dad and dad to mom and back and forth several times. They weren't looking anywhere except at their plates.

Suddenly, I knew one thing, I couldn't stand the study hall atmosphere any longer. "I sent away for hockey camp brochures."

Mom glanced up. "You did?"

"Haven't gotten any replies yet. Steve told me about some good camps."

"Meaning expensive ones," Dad said. "He lives on Newman Lane, doesn't he? Old money houses."

"Are we paupers?" Mom said.

He didn't answer.

"Don't worry. I'll pick the most reasonable one."

"I've heard that before," Mom said. "Reasonable like the cost of your hockey equipment? And for what? You never get in a game!"

I was beginning to be sorry I started a conversation but I said, "I played last week and I'll play again this weekend."

She put down her fork and stared at me.

"If you ever came to a game, maybe you'd know if I got to play," I said sullenly. Mom and dad not attending games never phased me before. I wasn't sure it *really* did now but I felt obligated to say something in reply to mom's steady gaze.

Mom seemed obligated to ignore those remarks. Instead she asked, "What about the dog?"

"What dog, Mom?"

She smiled, a smile which meant, "You know perfectly well what I'm talking about, Sarah, but if you want to be obstinate and childish, fine with me." Her voice said, "You wanted a dog this spring, didn't you?"

"Don't put it in the past tense! I still want one. I plan to go to the animal shelter the day the season ends."

"And another hockey season begins at summer camp," Dad said.

"So? I'll only be gone a few weeks."

"A dog is a big responsibility, Sarah. Dogs aren't as independent as Sir Lancelot. They require a lot of looking after."

"And from what I understand, Sarah," Mom said between bites of her hamburger, "you just might end up in summer school, not summer camp."

Again, I looked from one to the other. *What was going on?* Sounded like double-talk! I can't have a dog because I want to go to hockey school. I can't go to hockey school because I'll have a dog. And maybe I can't go anyway because I'll be in summer school! I also got the feeling that even though I was here, the conversation was really between my parents. Couldn't help but think of the Steinbergs. Had they started the same way? By being spiteful to Gayle? I couldn't swallow another french fry so I excused myself.

On Friday, I went to the library. Less than two weeks to read a three hundred page, maroon-colored book. David Underwood was at a table. I sat next to him. "Do you rent out space in libraries?"

"You're funny. I saw Gayle."

"Oh."

"Her parents are splitting up."

"She told you?"

He nodded. Good! At least it wasn't a secret anymore. Some secrets are wonderful to keep; this one was horrible.

"Are you looking for a book?" he asked.

"Yeah. I have to read something for English. And none of the books on the list have been movies."

He laughed. "You *are* funny, Sarah Dunes! Do you have the list with you?"

I pulled out the mimeographed sheet. As he read it over and kept nodding, I got the feeling David knew every book in the library, including the ones in the foreign language section. He's one of those genius types who also happens to be human. I hoped Gayle started seeing him again once her problems straightened out. If one's parents getting a divorce can ever get straightened out.

"When does the report have to be in?"

"Before Christmas vacation."

He gave a low whistle. "Not much time for you."

"Thanks!"

"Didn't mean to put you down." He reddened. "All I meant was you have hockey practice and all those games and well, most of these books are long."

"I know. Hey, are any of them condensed by *Reader's Digest* or one of the women's magazines?"

"No." David stopped blushing and continued reading the mimeographed sheet. "This one is good. And it's only two hundred pages."

" 'Only two hundred pages,' he says!" I sighed and rested my head on the table.

"According to *The New York Times*, it's going to be made into a movie this spring."

David knew everything! I raised my head. "The report does have to be written like a movie review but I don't think Mrs. Jacobs would give me that long an extension."

"You're something, Sarah."

"Yeah, something weird."

He got thoughtful looking. "Listen, after your paper is handed in, I could have it run in *Cross Words*. . . ."

"Felicity Cross hates me!"

Several people, including a librarian, warned us to "Ssh!"

"Felicity hates most people. Except you. You, I think she's afraid of. What did you say to her that day?"

I leaned over the table and whispered, "There are some things better left unsaid."

David grinned. "I'll take your word for it but Sarah,

Felicity loves good stuff in her paper. And a preview re- view of an upcoming film (even if it is a book review), she'd love that!"

"David, I have never pulled more than a C+ on my reports for Mrs. Jacobs."

"That's because you don't usually finish the book. This one is short, well, shorter than the rest, and really good—"

"Why don't you do the preview review then?"

"Because I'm asking you to do it. C'mon, Sarah! Think about showing Felicity up for that article . . ."

That hit the proper nerve. I agreed and we shook on it. I thanked David for his help and found the book. Two hundred pages didn't equal thin to me but the cover was intriguing—various shades of orange and yellow with scrawls of black writing and it all came together in an ab- stract skeleton's face. A scary book. I smiled. Not bad, not bad at all. I also found a couple of books on dog care.

Dad was home; mom wasn't. My stomach felt queasy. *Why did I keep thinking of Mr. Steinberg and his working late?*

"I was looking over the guest room earlier. Had to air it out."

For a crazy moment, I had visions of dad moving into the guest room. Permanently. Then I remembered. Aunt Rosiland's visit. Thank goodness!

I carried my books upstairs, making wet footprints (it

was snowing again) on the stairs. After I wiped up the mess, I walked into the kitchen. "What are you sketching?"

"The boutique made a deal with an Italian designer to have a special showing of his clothes. I'm doing some roughs for window displays."

I wondered if mom would be terribly thrilled. After all, the same designer probably sold to Greymer & Greymer. Don't think the big bosses in the city would appreciate their suburban manager's husband creating a smashing window display for the competition. And dad's work is a lot better than anything anyone at Greymer could come up with.

"If this keeps up, Sarah, I'll quit my real estate job in a few months."

"Fantastic!" Although he's good at it, dad hates selling houses.

"I sold some property I showed last week. Nice commission. Figured I'd put it in the bank for your summer hockey camp. I know how much going to one means to you."

I looked down at my large feet, not knowing what to say. Parents can surprise you.

"By the way," Dad said, grinning from ear to ear. "Steve called. He's coming over in awhile."

"*Dad!*" I screeched. Sir L hissed and ran for shelter under the couch. "How could you? Why didn't you tell him I had a date? It is *Friday* night, you know."

"Because you don't have a date," Dad said matter-of-factly. "Obviously, Steve doesn't, either, or he wouldn't be coming over."

"Rats!" I said in my best Charlie Brown manner.

"How's your leg?" I asked when Steve arrived (dad disappeared upstairs). "Haven't seen you in school."

"I stayed out a few days," he said, following me into the kitchen. "But it's fine now. No more stiffness."

"Yeah, that's what happened to my shoulder. Hurt at first and then it was like it'd never happened. Want some cocoa?" Dad had put the kettle on; I hadn't thought of it.

"Great. You did a super job filling in for me."

I tried not to blush. Have you ever tried *not* to blush? Take it from me, it's not something you can control!

"We're still right in the thick of it," Steve said. "If we'd lost that one, we would've been in real trouble. The Tornadoes are coming on strong. They're only two points behind us."

"So I noticed."

"When they creamed us the last time, it wasn't a fluke."

I was at the stove, checking on the kettle. I looked over my shoulder at Steve. His eyes darted everywhere. He reminded me of Sir L when Sir L's planning some mischief.

"Are you sure you're okay?" I asked, managing to pour two cups of boiling water without splattering any on the table or on Steve.

"Told you, my injury's just fine. Uh, I'm just nervous." Before I could ask him about what, he said, "I'm always jumpy the night before a game."

"You don't have to be," I said confidently. "I'll keep those Tornadoes in line!"

He was picking up his cup when I said that. Slowly, ever so slowly, he placed it back on the table. "*You'll* keep them in line?"

"Sure."

"Sarah, *I'm* the first-string goaltender."

I didn't like to hear that. I suddenly knew why he was here. "Break it to her gently, Steve. She actually believes she's going to get the starting nod. Poor Sarah Dunes, Weird Person." I could almost hear him saying it.

"But I deserve a shot!" I shouted. I hadn't intended to yell or to stand up and tower over a sitting Steve but I did.

"Cool it," he whispered.

"The only thing that'll cool is my cocoa when I come back here to drink it—*after you've gone!*"

"Sarah, I didn't mean—I'm really sorry."

"Please leave. Don't gloat in front of me. You're only getting the start because you're a boy!"

"Wait a minute, Sarah. Coach Caplan was the one who told me I'd start—"

I was halfway up the stairs by then. Dad stood in front of his bedroom door.

"What's all the commotion about?" he demanded.

"I should have introduced him to Susie—formally or informally!" I yelled at my totally bewildered father.

"Lower your voice, Sarah!" Dad thumbed to the bottom of the stairs. "Your guest might hear."

"I didn't invite him here. You did; therefore, he's *your* guest. I'm going to my room!"

I turned on the radio full blast and flopped on the bed. From every wall, Jim Craig's smiling face appeared. Suddenly, I hated him! Rhonda was right. I was being discriminated against! Quickly, the photographs were ripped down.

Once they covered my floor like a glossy rug, I returned to the bed. Absently, I picked up the book for English and opened to page one. Come tomorrow, I'd tell off Mr. Darrow, Coach Caplan, all the boys on the team, and even Piggy Barnes. I'd show them!

I wondered if the library would charge me for tear-stained pages.

14

W e've had more shots on goal than nine," Coach Caplan said, leaning over me during the third period of the Tornado game.

I shrugged and waved the clipboard. "Okay, how many? Fifteen? 1,045? Hey, I like that number!" And I started to write it down. While I hadn't told anyone off as planned, I hadn't exactly been sociable this morning.

She grabbed my clipboard. "I'll keep the tally. I'll continue to do so until you decide you're part of the team, Sarah Dunes."

"Girls aren't a part of *this* team," I muttered. It didn't help my cause any when, at the exact moment I uttered those words, Piggy Barnes scored a shorthanded goal.

En route home, after the 5–2 win, I spied Connie. She was walking toward the village, reading a script.

"We have a rehearsal for the Christmas pageant," she explained. "I get to narrate the whole thing. I think they picked me because my voice is the loudest. Even if the mike goes, the parents in the back rows will still hear me."

"Whoopee." Rehearsals meant I'd be seeing less and less of Connie again. And I only saw Gayle in school lately.

"Sarah, you look grim. Did you have a fight with a boy?"

Because she's not allowed to date, Connie thinks boys are the most important things in life; it can really be exasperating sometimes, like now. I told her briefly about Steve and how he got the starting bid over me. She listened, tsked, nodded, mmmed but didn't interrupt.

"Isn't that lousy? It's not fair at all!"

"Sarah," Connie's voice was low but urgent. She was standing next to me, talking directly into my armpits. "This is a blessing in disguise. What mama would call, 'God working in a mysterious way.' Hockey's too dangerous. You've been lucky so far. The only time you got hurt was in practice."

"The *only* time I play is in practice!"

"And even that was trouble. Look what kind of an animal ran into you. Piggy Barnes. Even her name is animalistic!"

"Did you know it's that way for real? The kids who've known her since kindergarten say her mother didn't know how to spell Peggy," I said, hoping to distract Connie and get her onto another topic. As usual, I should've known better.

"Sarah, she's still horrible! Do you really want to associate with girls like that? Do you want to become like her?" She didn't stop for a breath so I couldn't reply. "She tried to kill you and she's on your own team! Imagine what someone else might do! Sarah Dunes, do you want to lose all your teeth?"

"Teeth again!" I yanked the ends of my hair until my head hurt. "You make me feel like the lead in *Jaws!* I'm not particularly worried about my teeth; my parents certainly aren't. No one is, in fact, except for you and Dr. Marangi. His concern I can understand."

Connie's tone was urgent again. "Sarah, no boy wants to kiss a girl with false teeth."

Boys again. Might have known! "What about the cotton you stick in your bra?"

Connie blushed. "It isn't the same thing and you know it!"

I wasn't in the mood for a debate. This time I was going to change the subject. "What time do we start this great Christmas shopping expedition?"

"The stores open at eleven. I figure we can all meet on Collier."

I nodded, wished her luck with her rehearsal, and hurried away before she could change the subject again.

I watched *Godzilla*, which was followed by a Marx Brothers film. The latter was still on when mom walked in.

"Do you really think *A Night at the Opera* will help you pass science?"

My parents knew all about the 53 percent by now. "Groucho has an answer for everything. If I watch the movie long enough, maybe he'll say something that'll help—"

Mom pulled the plug on the set. "Hit the books."

"I'm hungry."

She glanced around the room. Behind those thick eyeglasses sit eagle-eyes. Besides, it was hard to hide the yogurt cups and two bags of pretzels, not to mention a container of milk.

"Study for an hour. Dinner will be ready then. If you can find room for it," she said smugly.

"Okay, I guess I'd rather get the junk out of the way tonight. Have a busy day tomorrow."

"Doing what?"

She sounded like a lemon again.

"I'm going Christmas shopping with Connie and Gayle."

"No."

"What?"

"You heard me, Sarah. You're not going anywhere tomorrow. You're going to spend the day studying. And don't you have a book report due?"

"Yeah, but I'm reading the book. It's great! It's all about this supposedly dead—"

"Spare me the gory details. Forget about the shopping trip tomorrow. The day Christmas vacation begins, you can come with me to the store and get what you want, using my discount. If Connie and Gayle want to come along, they're welcome. In fact, I'll even spring for lunch at Greymer Gardens. I am not an ogre, Sarah."

Greymer Gardens is a fancy restaurant on the top floor of the store, down the hall from mom's plush office. They cut the sandwiches in fours, cut off the crust, and fill them with paper-thin strips of inedible chicken salad. They also serve overly sweet eclairs and waxy tasting petit fours. I'd rather eat my own cooking.

Monday was another typically rotten day, with *Miz* Mitchum criticizing my workshirt, even though it was the best in the class. I also think I flunked another science test. I hid in the bathroom before leaving. I was in no mood to face a sullen, happy, or in-between Gayle. When I figured the halls would be empty, I ventured out. Unfortunately, Alex Smythe was on late monitor patrol, making sure the students had cleared out before the janitor came up.

"When's the next hockey game?"

"Just before New Year's. Since when are you interested in sports?"

"Since the gym teacher gave me a special assignment. It's the only way he'll pass me, Sarah. I have to attend a school sport within the next two weeks and hand in a report on it. Dumb, huh?"

"I dunno. If it'll help you pass . . ."

"That was just what I was hoping you'd say, Sarah. I can read about the game in the newspaper but I gotta have a *stub* to prove I went to the game—"

"No way! I'm not going to get you a stub. Go to the game. You might learn something." I marched down the hall.

"C'mon! Gimme a break!" Alex pleaded, galloping after me. "I got more important things to do on Christmas vacation than going to a lousy hockey game. I could be sleeping!"

I stopped short. Naturally, Alex couldn't brake in time. I could also stand my ground; he couldn't. I looked at him sprawled on the floor, his patrol monitor armband had slipped to his wrist. "You see a hockey game. I probably flunk science again. Things are tough all over."

Then I helped him up and readjusted his armband.

"You're not only tall, Sarah, you're weird. Really *weird.*"

"My theme song," I said and raced out of the building.

A heavy snow pelted down. Some kids were sitting on snow-covered cars singing off-key versions of "White Christmas" and "Silent Night." Pretty soon, you wouldn't be able to distinguish between the cars and the kids. But there was one person I could identify. Gayle was standing slightly apart from the singers. She was obviously waiting for me; all my hiding in the smelly bathroom hadn't helped. I sighed and managed a smile.

"How'd you do on the science test?"

"Who knows? Sedimentary rocks, metamorphic rocks, stalagmites, stalactites . . . kind of blends together after a while."

"I think I passed," Gayle said.

"Of course! You're a straight A student in science."

"I haven't pulled an A in anything lately."

How could I have forgotten? All those days out of school. I stared at her; Gayle's pretty face was thin and mean-looking. "Did you go shopping with Connie?" I asked, as we plodded through the snow. It was up to my ankles already.

"Yeah."

"What did you get your folks for Hanukkah?" Like a dummy I asked that! I wished the snow was deep enough for me to burrow into.

Gayle just shrugged. "For mom, I bought a lovely shawl. Absolutely gorgeous! I didn't get a thing for *him*."

From the way she said it, the more convinced I was she wasn't any too thrilled with her father. After all, he'd been the one to have the affair and bust up the marriage. But the bitterness in her voice sent shivers down my spine. You know, the kind you get right before Anthony Perkins stabs Janet Leigh in the shower scene in *Psycho* (even if you've seen the film nine times like I have).

"Mom's letting me loose in Greymer. Want to come along?"

She didn't answer.

"I'd love the company. Mom'll be too busy to bother with me. She's been working awfully hard. Comes home real late almost every night."

"Late?"

I stared down at Gayle. She sounded positively gleeful!

"Yeah, late!"

"Sarah," she whispered, sounding urgent like Connie. "That doesn't sound right."

"Why not?" I said irritably. "My mom's the manager and it is the holiday season—"

But Gayle wasn't really listening to me. "He told my mother he had to work late every night because things were busy at the office. That was *his* story, too."

"But my mom's telling the truth!"

Gayle's eyes flickered. "Mmmm . . ."

We were at our usual parting spot. I said good-bye and she "mmmed" again. For some reason, my heart raced. Well, for a specific reason. I had been worried about mom. Working late, that rotten scene at dinner the other night, and mom and dad not talking the way they used to.

Stop it, Sarah! That's Gayle's problem!

I hurried down Waverly, almost tripping over the crumbled sidewalk. No one was home, for which I was thankful. I sat on the bathroom floor. Thought I wanted to cry but the tears wouldn't come. Sir L padded in and stretched out next to me. "I want a dog," I told him, scratching him behind the ears. He purred. "But you're one terrific cat. I'll be sure to get a dog you approve of."

He continued to purr contentedly. I still couldn't cry. I felt like I was going to explode.

Before mom left for work the next day, she told me, "Rosiland's due this afternoon. The snow's stopped so her plane from Florida should be able to land. She's coming straight here from the airport. I won't be home and neither will your father. He's busy with his precious Veronique Boutique, aren't you, Winston?"

He was on the living room couch, sketching. He didn't even bother to look up.

"Don't hang around at school."

"I never hang around, Mom! You know that!" Unless one counted hiding in the bathroom. I didn't.

"There's always a first time." Then she laughed. "Sarah, stop looking so serious!"

I tried to catch my reflection in the bay window but the sun glared on it. Did I look serious? And if I did, did it matter?

"Entertain your aunt."

"What?"

Mom buttoned her tweed coat. "Sarah, I do not mean entertain as in balancing a ball on your nose. Just be your usual charming self."

"Your sarcasm has been noted," I mumbled.

A little after four, the doorbell rang. I ran to answer it then stopped dead in my tracks. I haven't seen Aunt Rosiland in a couple of years. Suppose I let a stranger into the house? Visions of the Avon lady trying to sell me bubble bath danced in my head. Oh, well, I could always give them to Piggy and Felicity as Christmas gifts. I opened the door.

"Dammit! You look just like Rhonda!"

A tall, heavy woman blocked the whole doorway. She was hatless and her hair was short and pepper-and-salt colored. She also had the widest grin I've ever seen. Aunt Rosiland was thinner and had black hair. The Rosiland I remembered, anyhow. But that smile was a dead giveaway . . .

"Lady, where do ya want these?"

"A New York cabbie!" I hollered happily. "You're an endangered species!"

Aunt Rosiland had moved and I could see the driver. He gave me a nasty look and mumbled something about kids being seen and not heard.

"In the hallway here," Aunt Rosiland told him.

He did and she paid him, obviously tipping him big because he kept saying thanks, thanks and tipping his battered leather cap.

"All the way up here," she said slamming the door, "that gnome smoked the smelliest cigar!"

"Hello, Aunt Rosiland."

She hugged me. "Hello to you, too, Sarah Dunes."

"Do you want me to lug your bags upstairs? Or do you want a drink or do you have to use the bath—"

"The last. Where is it?"

"Down the hall and to the left," I said pointing.

She went and kept yakking in her booming voice. "Open the green suitcase. No, not the leather one!" she said, knowing which one I'd headed for (even if she couldn't see me). "The canvas one. Your gifts are in there."

I tried to lift the canvas bag. "Ouuff!" I wondered how the gnome had managed to do it without getting a hernia. I knelt on the floor and tackled it that way. Nice and heavy. What kind of gift would be nice and heavy?

Books.

"Your mother says you don't read."

"I do so read!" I yelled back. "I just don't read what she wants me to. I'm reading the last chapter of this great scary novel. Oh, no," I muttered. The books were old, fat, and nubby-linen covered.

"I know they look intimidating but they're really terrific."

I glanced up. Aunt Rosiland stood there, pulling her girdle around her ample waist. She didn't strike me as the sort of person who'd be intimidated by anything, let alone a book. But she was. I was beginning to think I'd found someone I might be able to talk to when she said, "If they, the books, unnerve you that much, I'll read aloud to you. That'll be fun, won't it?"

No self-respecting thirteen year old would allow an adult to read to them! I wasn't a little kid like Jimmy! Aunt Rosiland didn't understand at all. The only way I'd let her read to me would be if I was forced to. You know, like flat on my back or something.

How she knew "something" was imminent, I'll never understand.

15

As it turned out, Aunt Rosiland didn't require much entertaining. She said she'd change her clothes and get into something more comfortable. I led her to the guest room, which she liked. That's when I realized she'd never seen our house. On the last every-other-Christmas, we'd still lived in the city.

"Want the grand tour?" I asked while Sir L twitched his whiskers at her red clogs.

"No, we'll leave that for tomorrow." She threw on a paisley caftan that made her look like a medium-sized sofa. "I'll watch TV. Do whatever it is you do when I'm not here."

There was a gory Vincent Price movie on. She spread her paisley self on our checked couch. She asked me when mom and dad would be home and I told her I didn't know.

"No big deal but I just hope they get here before Rhonda does."

"Huh?"

She grinned her enormous smile again. "I called my little sister from the airport. I'm dying to see her. Can't get over how much you look like her."

"My nose is too short."

"You look like her, short nose or not. What's this fellow like?"

"Darling? He's great! He took us to a Ranger game."

She roared and the vibrations caused me to flop on a handy chair. "Rhonda and Darling! At a hockey game, no less! Will wonders never cease?"

I didn't see what was so hysterical and frankly, Aunt Rosiland grated on my nerves. I excused myself, picked myself out of the chair, and went upstairs. I finished reading the final chapter of the scary book and wrote my movie-style review, giving the book four stars.

I returned downstairs just as the six o'clock news was going off and dad was walking in. To my surprise, he hugged Aunt Rosiland. I guess he liked her. Better than Rhonda; anyhow, he only had to see Rosiland once every two years.

He'd brought home Chinese food and chocolate eclairs. While I stuffed myself with *bok choy*, they chatted about the weather, their jobs, the economy, politics, and other dull subjects.

Then Aunt Rosiland turned to me. "Maybe I'll see you in goal while I'm here."

I sipped green tea. "I doubt it. Steve Hollaway has a lock on that position."

"Oh."

It's hard to judge an "Oh" when it's uttered by someone you don't know that well. Yet her voice was loaded with meaning. Was she yet another person who had my future all laid out for me?

"You did a beautiful job on the tree, Winston."

Dad beamed and I mean beamed! In most homes I know, the kids get to decorate the tree or at least help. Not here. Dad's particular about the art of trimming.

We have a fake six-footer that stands just to the right of the bay window and to the left of the TV. There's oodles of tinsel, each strand carefully hung so that each branch holds four strands, no more, no less. And the lights are tiny twinkling stars, strung in green-yellow-red-yellow-blue, in that order. The tree is topped with a breathtaking silver and gold star created by dad himself. Our Christmas tree is lovelier than any storefront tree and especially prettier than any tree in Greymer & Greymer (either in the city or suburban branches), which drives mom crazy.

"We pay a fortune to the window dresser at the store and my own husband can do this!"

"Pay me a fortune and I'll gladly do Greymer's."

They had that dialogue every year and every year, after they said it, they'd embrace each other. They didn't have that conversation this year. They also haven't done much hugging.

A car pulled into the driveway. I dashed to the window. The porch light shone brightly but not on mom's green compact. *Why is she working so late?*

When I opened the door, Rhonda bounced in. She wore a fantastic floor-length, black velvet cape.

"Do you love it? Do you absolutely love it?" She whirled around, looking like an ad for a *Dracula's Daughter* film.

"Beautiful," I mumbled, touching the soft material.

"Darling gave it to me. An early gift, you know."

And as if on cue, he walked in, looking as handsome as I'd remembered. "Merry Christmas, Sarah Dunes."

"Yeah, Merry-Merry." Which wasn't the way I felt.

Rhonda flung off her cape and it neatly caught on the bannister knob. If I'd tried that, it would have fallen to the floor and Sir L would've promptly made a bed of it.

Underneath the cape, she wore a silky red jump suit. I don't look like her! It's like saying Peppermint Patty and Wonder Woman are twins.

"Rosiland, darling, Rosiland!" Rhonda said, swooping over to her oldest sister. "Should we tell them now, Darling? Of course not! Roxanne's not here yet!"

"And I haven't the faintest idea when she will be, either."

Dad's voice was flat. He wasn't overjoyed at playing host to mom's family without mom.

"Okay, okay," Rhonda said, jangling silver bracelets as she spoke. "No formal announcements until Roxanne gets here."

I tiptoed over. "I'm informal."

She giggled and Aunt Rosiland, who was now watching a noisy game show, rolled her eyes.

"Okay, just you, Sarah. We're getting, uh, you know."

"Married?" I squeaked.

"Yes, Sarah! Can you believe it? Darling's going to ask Win about the houses on the market up here."

"Commuting to the city is hard from here," I said, sitting on the arm of the couch.

"Commuting?" Rhonda's face was blank for a second, then she smiled. "Sarah, don't be silly! He's not going to commute! Darling's getting a post with one of those sleepy little colleges up here."

"Oh. But what about your career?"

She blinked and her eyelashes touched her upper lip. "Sarah, I'm unemployed!"

"But you went to school for engineering. There aren't many engineering jobs up here. I don't think so—"

"Oh, *that!*" Her bracelets clinked again. "That's a whole other life ago. I have a new career—"

"Here it comes," Aunt Rosiland muttered.

"—I'm going to be a professor's wife!" She giggled.

"Sarah, I can hardly wait to pick out a house! You know, a little cottage-type with a picket fence."

I couldn't think of a thing to say, other than to inquire if my Aunt Rhonda had been possessed by another being since what this person was saying was completely the opposite from what Rhonda usually said. Fortunately, or so I thought at the moment, the door opened and mom waltzed in.

"Hi there, folks!"

"About time," Dad muttered.

Mom hung up her tweed coat in the hall closet, which reminded me, my coat, the one with the button still missing, was underneath Rhonda's cape.

"The clan has gathered! Greetings!" Mom said.

When she walked by me, I smelled booze. Mom only drinks at parties. An office party! Here we are, waiting for her, and she's enjoying herself somewhere else! I had a hunch dad wouldn't appreciate that one bit—I was right.

He pulled her into the corner, by the fridge, and began talking in hushed tones. I ambled over. "Now that you're here, Rhonda wants to make an announcement."

Mom nodded impatiently. The whole of her face was pinker than the blusher she wore. "I know, I know. She's going to marry what's-his-face. It's not a bad face." She giggled.

"How'd you know?"

"Sarah, go away. Your mother and I have to talk."

"What's the matter? Do I have the plague?"

I must've really yelled because Rhonda and Darling stopped cooing and Aunt Rosiland actually turned off the set. All eyes on me made me even angrier. I felt like I was going to explode. I kept yelling.

"You know, I've been thinking how weird I am. I've been thinking so long and so hard that weird is about all I do think about lately!" I paused and looked at five startled adult faces. "But it never hit me until just now that *you're* the weird ones!"

"Sarah, cut it out!" Dad snapped.

"Don't get so excited!" Rhonda said.

"Why should I cut it out and why shouldn't I get so excited?" I demanded, thumping my flat chest. "Everyone's been so busy telling me how weird I am because I play hockey and how no one will want to kiss a girl with false teeth. Well, I think Connie's weird because she's never been out with a boy. And Gayle—" I pulled at my hair.

"Sarah, please sit down," Rhonda said.

"Yes, sit down," Dad said softly.

The calmer they were, the more heated I became. I knew I was exploding but I couldn't stop it. Mostly, I didn't want to. "I will not! I'm going to stand right here! Why should I listen to anything you have to say, anyway, Rhonda? I believed your feminist talk and it was all a lie! You just shot off your mouth so why can't I?"

I was crying now. All this rotten stuff had been inside me for so long! Coach Caplan lying to me about playing. Piggy Barnes nearly killing me because I was supposed to have asked Steve to a dance that I didn't ask him to in the first place! And Felicity Cross writing that horrible column and . . .

"And why do you keep working late?" I whirled to mom. She was leaning against the refrigerator. "You never worked such long hours before. You're just like Mr. Steinberg, aren't you? And dad, you're working for that snotty boutique! Why? Why's everybody doing what they're doing?"

The only sound in the house was that of my own heartbeat. It sounded like a cavalry thundering across the plains. Then everything became horribly blurred. The Christmas tree lights blended in with Rhonda's silver jewelry and that blended in with the fluorescent kitchen light.

"I can't see you but I bet you're all still staring at me!" I cried. "And you're still thinking, 'Wow, Sarah Dunes is one Weird Person,' but I'm not! *I'm not!*"

And with a final screech, I ran into the hall and grabbed a coat off the bannister. I flew out the door. Everyone shouted after me but I bounded up Waverly.

And as I raced up bumpy, slippery Waverly in what turned out to be Rhonda's long, wide cape, my foot hit a patch of extremely slick ice.

That's when I fell flat on my face.

16

The next few hours were hazy. I remember coming to and hearing Steve Hollaway's voice. How and why he came to be on Waverly didn't become clear until much later, however.

"Stay put, Sarah. I'll get your folks. Stay put."

Did he expect me to get up and do wind sprints?

Then there were a whole bunch of voices. Mom's rang out above the others. "Win, don't move her! You're not supposed to move the body!"

I wanted to argue that I didn't exactly qualify as a "body" body but the words wouldn't come out. That's when I tasted the blood. I wasn't frightened by it; I merely passed out.

When I woke up again, mom's voice was considerably softer. She was saying something about stitches and eyebrows. Even in my semifog, my stomach rebelled. I gurgled.

Someone patted my mouth and a somewhat familiar

woman's voice said, "I'm afraid there's nothing we can do about her teeth tonight."

Teeth?

"That's a job for her dentist."

I ran my tongue over my top teeth. Except they weren't there. My two front teeth felt like a tiny sideways Z. The rest of the upper teeth felt all right. Gingerly, I tried for the bottom teeth. Several were chipped.

"I did it," I murmured.

"Sarah, you're awake! You're in the emergency room!" Mom's voice was ringing again.

"Did it."

"Did what, Sarah?"

"Wrecked my teeth. Everyone said . . ."

"Forget about what people said, Sarah. Just rest."

I kept tickling the Z with the tip of my tongue and dozed off.

They must've gotten me home and into my pajamas because I next awoke in the morning and was in my own bed. When I climbed out of bed, my head bonged. I considered crawling back under the covers but getting to the bathroom was more pressing than the pain.

After finishing what I had to do in the bathroom, I struggled to the medicine chest and stared into the mirror. A funny thing happened. Sarah Dunes did not reflect back. In her place was a scrawny prizefighter, complete with black eyes, large bandage across the right eyebrow, a smaller bandage on a pug nose, and smashed up teeth.

I kept peering at the beat-up face and slowly, oh-so-slowly, I realized, Sarah Dunes was the prizefighter.

"Mom! Dad!" I squeaked.

Somehow, they heard me. Mom put her arms around my shoulders. "It's okay, Sarah," she said, directing me back to my room. "You'll be fine."

"I look ugly," I whimpered. The whimper turned into a wail and I cried like a baby.

The doorbell rang. Dad went down, came back up, went through my desk, then left again, something clutched in his hand. By now I'd stopped crying. My eyes were too sore. Then Aunt Rosiland waltzed in, toting a tray of toast, tea, and orange juice.

"You can dunk the toast," she said.

"Why's there a straw in the juice?" I asked. Only most of that question came out as an enormous lisp. With the condition my mouth was in, there was no way I could drink without a straw. As soon as the herbal tea cooled, I used the straw on that, too.

I slept the remainder of the day. It wasn't until the next morning that I ventured downstairs. When Aunt Rosiland suggested she read aloud to me from one of the books she'd brought, I wasn't insulted. In fact, I liked the idea. She had a good read-to voice and the story was terrific. It was all about this poor English kid, Tom Canty and Tudor Prince Edward, who switch identities. It's called *The*

Prince and the Pauper. Aunt Rosiland was surprised I hadn't seen the movie on TV. The book and the film were her favorites. The Lady Jane Grey was about to walk into the prince's chambers where Tom had assumed Edward's identity when the doorbell rang. I was to have several visitors in the next few days.

As disappointed as I was to have story hour interrupted, I was delighted to see Connie and Gayle.

"Merry Christmas!" I called (lisping all the time) from my perch on the couch. "Oh, you shouldn't have gotten me anything." I pointed to the brightly wrapped gifts in their hands. "I haven't had a chance to shop."

"Don't be silly," Gayle said, putting the presents under the tree.

She was still subdued, I noted, but at least she managed to come over. Maybe that was a hopeful sign? I introduced them to my aunt and Rosiland left us alone.

No one said anything for awhile. Gayle studied the tree but Connie was much more direct. She gaped at my face.

"I know; I look like Rocky."

She reddened and turned her attention to the wall. "It looks like it hurts a lot. Will you have to have them out?"

"My black eyes?"

"Sarah Dunes!" She looked back at me and grinned.

I grinned, too, and even detected a slight smile on Gayle's face. "If you mean my teeth, probably. Dr. Marangi won't be in his office until after Christmas."

"Well, you won't have to wait long for new ones, Sarah," Connie said. "You'll have impressions made the same day you have the teeth yanked and the impressions are sent out to a lab—"

"Impressions?" Gayle wrinkled her nose.

"Yeah, the dentist puts yuckky pink gunk in your mouth and you press down on it. I read all about it in hygiene."

"Spare us, Connie," Gayle said.

I nodded in agreement. They understood about my being sleepy and they left a few minutes later. I swore I would not peek at the presents until Christmas morning. But before going to my room for a nap, I did rattle the packages. It didn't give me a clue.

Mom was sitting on the edge of the bed when I woke up. After she asked how I was, she said, "You were right about you not being the only one who was acting weird."

"I was?" I asked, sitting up.

"I did my share of 'weirdo-ing,' " Mom said. "You have no idea how ticked off I was at your father because he accepted that job with Veronique Boutique. Even though it was only a part-time job."

"Because they're your main competition."

"No, Sarah. That's the strange part. I could've cared less about it being Greymer's rival. I'd hoped my big promotion would enable your father to devote all his time to cartooning. I was putting in all sorts of overtime in order to make certain this was the biggest and best Christmas

146

season the suburban store ever had *and* I hoped I'd get a fat bonus so I'd have ready cash for your hockey school—"

I grinned. "Dad already got the money. From a commission on a house."

"See, I didn't even know that. Everything would've been a lot simpler if I'd leveled with him and vice versa. There is one question, Sarah. Why am I like Mr. Steinberg?"

I told her and she said it was too bad about Gayle's parents but divorces do happen.

"But they're not happening to your dad and me."

"Don't worry. I get it now," I said happily.

"Good. Don't be too hard on Rhonda, either."

I stopped being happy. "She's nothing but a phony! All her talk—"

Mom held up her hand. "That's just it. Talk. Sarah, people say a lot of things they don't mean. Rhonda thought feminism was fashionable and Rhonda is always fashionable. Maybe she was a little jealous, too, of the topflight jobs Ros and I have. But I think all along she wanted to be a housewife, which is a career in itself, you know."

"Of course I do!"

"My bright daughter does but it took my daffy younger sister awhile to comprehend." Mom laughed then said, "By the way, I saw David Underwood at the mall. He liked your movie review-book report, whatever that is."

"He did? Does he have x-ray vision into this house? I haven't been to school."

That's when I found out what dad had been doing in my desk the morning after the accident. David's mother, Dr. Underwood, had been that semifamiliar voice in the emergency room. She told him what had happened and he'd come by for the report.

"Good thing, too," I said. "With my track record, I don't think Mrs. Jacobs would've believed my accident."

"He also said his offer still stands. Something about Felicity quitting and he taking over?" Mom looked at me quizzically.

"That's a surprise. The staff must've mutinied." So, my report would actually appear in David's newspaper! A nice surprise. I was in for another surprise.

On Christmas Eve, my parents went out for a special Italian dinner (promising to doggy-bag several garlic flavored breadsticks for me. I could eat a little better now). Aunt Rosiland retired to her room while I read (my eyes were less sore and more open) *The Prince and the Pauper*. The doorbell rang. "I wonder who that is?" I said to Sir L who had curled up under the tree. He meowed softly. "Yeah, guess I have to answer it to find out."

Steve Hollaway didn't seem to be the least bit startled to see my bruised face. Probably because I'd looked a lot worse when he found me that night. But I was definitely startled to see him at my front door.

"Merry Christmas," we said at the same time. He smiled and I invited him in. He sat on a chair.

"I just came over to find out how you're doing," he mumbled. "And, uh, to confess something."

"Confessions of a First-string Goaltender. Sounds like a Rona Barrett scoop."

"Rona? Is she in your class?"

"Forget it," I said.

His face color matched the shade of his hair. He cleared his throat twice before finally speaking. "It's really what I came over to tell you the other night. The night you fell. It's about, uh, Piggy."

He stopped talking but continued to blush. Piggy? The way he was acting, I expected him to confess he was a member of the CIA! What could he possibly have to divulge about Piggy Barnes?

"Sarah, Piggy never asked me to the Topsy-Turvy Dance."

The Topsy-Turvy was another life ago, as Rhonda would say. But if Piggy hadn't invited Steve . . . "Wait a minute, she slammed into me that day in practice. That was in retaliation for going with you—"

"No, Sarah. Piggy crashed into you because she needed eyeglasses."

My mouth twitched like Sir L's whiskers. "She what?"

Steve nodded. "Didn't you notice all those shots she'd been missing awhile back?" This time I nodded; he continued, "My father's an optometrist in the village. I was in the store the day Piggy came in for an exam. When she found out she needed glasses, she tore out of there. Her parents dragged her back a few days later and she's wearing contacts now."

Which explained why Piggy's shots had been so off target, why she crashed into me, and why her shots were so right on goal now. What it didn't explain was why Steve asked me . . .

"I thought you, uh, were going to ask me to the dance," Steve said, getting redder. "When it got closer to the dance and you didn't, I, uh, well, I made up that story about Piggy."

We sat there real quiet for a couple of minutes. His confession coupled with his embarrassment were beginning to make sense. Steve liked me! Me, as a girl, not as a hockey player. And he still did, even with broken teeth!

"I'm glad you made up that story," I said shyly. I was even gladder I'd never introduced him to Susie. "And thanks for helping me the night I fell."

He stopped turning red and smiled. I smiled, too. When he left, I ran up to my room. The magazine photos of Jim Craig were still on the floor (although in a neat pile, courtesy of dad). I put them back up.

Two days after what turned out to be one of the best Christmases on record, I had an appointment with Dr.

Marangi. Mom and dad offered to escort me but I turned them down. I had to face the public with my face someday and that day might as well be now. The swelling on my eyes had lessened. I simply looked like I was celebrating Halloween out of season.

When Dr. Marangi saw me, he said, "Now I see why we needed an emergency visit. Did it happen during a game?"

I told him about the accident and didn't even bother to correct the "we."

"Ahhh," he said when I finished.

"That's my line."

He laughed but then spoke seriously, "The two on the top will have to come out, Sarah."

I expected as much but the reality still jolted me. "Will I have false teeth like those?" I pointed to a pair of choppers on the counter.

"Dear me, no! Sarah, you'll just have small plastic teeth. They will come out, though. When you're older and your back teeth come in, we can hook on a bridge. That will be stationary. Do you know what a bridge is, Sarah?"

I nodded. Aunt Rosiland had one. I'd ask her about it; she had told her business partner she was staying with us for a month. Rhonda's marriage was at the end of January. And Dr. Marangi was actually saying *you* instead of *we*, without any coaxing! He assured me the impressions could indeed be taken on the day of the extraction (which he scheduled for the next day).

"The new teeth will be in right after New Year's and I'll cap those bottom teeth in a matter of days, too. Don't worry, Sarah. You'll have a normal mouth in a few weeks."

Sarah Dunes, Normal Person? No, I wasn't ready for that yet. How about Sarah Dunes, Normally Weird Person? Mmmm, I could get used to the sound of that!

After graduating from business school, Lois I. Fisher worked in many fields, including fashion, magazine publishing, and construction. Her favorite was working on the construction site of a Manhattan skyscraper.

Her hobbies include watching sports, doing difficult crossword puzzles, and collecting rock records from the 1960s.

Stories by Lois Fisher have appeared in dozens of juvenile and young adult publications. This is her first novel. She has always lived in The Bronx, New York.